ßEHOLDEN
ÐUET

Zoey Ellis writes dark-edged fantasy romances described by readers as 'intensely erotic' and 'unputdownable.' A Londoner, cat mama, and proud romance and epic fantasy addict, Zoey loves possessive heroes, sexual tension that jumps off the page, and memorable, magical worlds. Visit her online home for more media and updates about her books and author journey: www.zoeyellis.com

A SAVAGE DEBT

BEHOLDEN DUET BOOK ONE

ZOEY ELLIS

A Savage Debt, Beholden Duet Book 1
Copyright © Zoey Ellis 2018. All rights reserved
www.zoeyellis.com

Zoey Ellis Books
ISBN: 978-1-912931-32-3

First Edition: April 2020

For Mum and Dad

ONE

"**H**e's here!"

A rough hand curled around Ana's elbow and tried to tug her up from her chair.

"Quick, Ana. We need to go."

Ana blinked rapidly, readjusting to her surroundings as she pulled her mind from the world contained in the thick book on her lap. "Milly?"

Her lady-in-waiting leaned over and closed her book as a group of guards fanned out to surround her chair. "Up, princess. We must leave now."

Ana rose slowly, a crack of anger suddenly charring the delightful calm she'd sunk into—that soothing peace that always came from visiting her library. "But, Milly, it is only just early morning, and I haven't been here long—"

"No arguments, Ana," Milly said briskly. Strands of her usually impeccable dark brown hair flailed around her head. "We cannot take any risks while he's here."

Ana frowned. "Who?"

Milly's voice sharpened as she turned to leave. "Make haste!"

She followed Milly out of the library, and the profanity forming in her mouth almost escaped her. It hummed between her lips, promising to satisfy the annoyance churning in her chest, if she'd only let it slip past them.

But princesses did not curse. Especially not a princess like Ana.

"Who's here?" she asked again.

Milly's head whipped around, her eyes narrowed. "Shh!"

Ana stared at the back of her head as she hurried after her, her irritation twisting into alarm. Milly had never acted so harshly before. Yes, she was stern, diligent, and protective—she'd practically raised Ana—but this behavior, particularly in public, was out of character. Something was wrong.

As they navigated the corridors toward her bed chambers, Ana realized the atmosphere in the palace had drastically changed since this morning, and not in a way she recognized.

No one openly spoke of it, but the high society of Allandis was a grotesque web of scandal, intimidation, and indecency. Every so often, a juicy bubble of gossip burst into the open, forcing the court nobility to pretend to be both outraged and disinterested while they secretly scrabbled for every morsel of information they could get.

Ana found it amusing at times. It changed the mood of the palace and caused the courtiers, the staff, and sometimes even the guards to behave inappropriately. Watching them entertained her most of the time, and gossip broke up the monotony of her schedule. Even though she never had access to the secrets circling, she'd learned a lot about high society, and the royal court, based on the behavior she'd witnessed—things that did not find its way into her lessons.

But this felt different. The haughty ambiance that characterized the palace was laced with a tang of tense agitation. Courtiers huddled in small clusters exchanging hushed words out in the open. Servants kept their eyes down and practically ran along the corridors—something that was expressly forbidden. And armed guards had been stationed at every corner, their bodies alert and eyes watchful.

Ana said nothing more until they arrived at her bed chambers.

"Forget the bath, start with her hair and face," Milly called as soon as they entered. Four handmaids were already inside, flitting around the room with tools in their hands that suggested to Ana she was being prepared for a court event.

"What's happening, Milly?" Ana asked, as Milly headed to her wardrobe. "Is this to do with Father?" The king had been critically injured while out on his last hunt a month ago. That was the only time the court had been justified in acting so panicked. Milly had come to collect her then also, only she'd been more subdued. Father had, thankfully, fully recovered, but Ana wasn't keen on any more news like that.

Milly approached her with an elaborate lavender dress while one of the handmaids unzipped her out of the one she wore. "There is to be a court assembly.

The whole court and the royal houses will be in attendance. We must get you prepared quickly."

Ana tried to question her further, but Milly was in a focused frenzy that somehow prevented her ears from working. For the next quarter of an hour, Milly and her handmaids groomed Ana more intensely than any other time she could remember, ignoring her questions in favor of discussions about clashing colors and matching jewelry.

Ana held in the steady annoyance building in her chest. Sometimes she wished she were brave enough to stomp around the palace and force everyone to listen to her, not caring if she offended anyone. She was frequently told how important she was—to her father, to her court, to the kingdom. Being an Omega automatically meant she was revered and even idolized, but in reality her *opinion* wasn't important. She used to think she would become more forceful, like her father, or cleverer with words, like her mother, but she realized she didn't possess those qualities. She'd never been brash or rude or reckless. Her upbringing had centered around meeting the expectations that weighed heavily on her, and since she didn't like disappointing Milly or her parents, she worked hard to please them. As a result, she was known as the perfect princess; her father's strongest asset and the kingdom's greatest treasure. If only she'd known the extent to which she would lack control of her own life… maybe then she would have behaved differently, taken more risks. Still, it wouldn't be this way forever. Next month she would marry an Alpha and a new phase of her life would begin, one where she would have more control.

Finally, Milly stepped back to survey her, and Ana tried again, her voice firm. "I wasn't aware of any event happening today, Milly. What is this one about? Is it a wedding announcement?"

Milly stepped forward again, lifting her hands to press smooth and fix Ana's newly styled rose-copper hair. "No. It's much bigger than that. It's to be the most important event in the history of the court."

Ana pursed her lips as she frowned. That was an interesting thing for Milly to say. Although Milly was always knowledgeable about court gossip, she rarely talked about it with Ana, and she certainly didn't make extravagant statements. "What is it then?"

Milly glanced at her and finally stilled. She stepped back and composed herself, though her eyes remained stained with an uneasy glint. With beautifully rich brown hair, deep blue eyes, and slightly leathery skin, it was difficult to guess Milly's age. She'd been Ana's lady-in-waiting since she could remember, and behaved like a stern older sister, a teacher, and sometimes even a mother, though she certainly wasn't as old as the queen. She constantly bristled, with her hard edges at the forefront, but she had her moments of softness. As a noble woman, Milly was well versed in royal procedure and politics, even if she didn't like to discuss every part of it with Ana. Regardless, Ana had learned a lot from her that she didn't learn from her mother and father, and sometimes it was from simply observing Milly's behavior.

"A criminal has arrived at the palace."

Ana's brows drew together. "That is a big event?"

"It's Maddoc."

A cold rush tingled up Ana's arms, and her lungs expelled a gust of air. "Maddoc? As in…"

Milly nodded. "There is only one Maddoc, Ana."

Ana stared at her, dread creeping into her throat. The most feared criminal known to the kingdom. The brutal, vicious Alpha who had eluded capture for over a decade while striking damaging blows to the royal sovereignty was at the palace? "Are you sure?" Her voice was raspy. "Why would he come here and allow himself to be captured?"

Milly shrugged, but the unease in her eyes remained. "He's demanded to see the king."

Suddenly it all fell into place—the behavior of the courtiers, the panicked servants, the rush to get ready for a court hearing. "Father is going to give him an audience? Here?" Ana squeaked. "Why?"

"I haven't been brought into discussions about that, of course," Milly said curtly "But I suspect it is to charge him in front of the assembly."

Ana shook her head, her mouth open in disbelief. Surely Father wouldn't risk that?

"It would be a great show of strength to arrest and charge this man in front of all the houses," Milly added. "The king needs to prove he is strong, powerful, and capable. Whatever reason this criminal chose to show up at the gates and whatever he is expecting, it must be demonstrated to all that the king isn't afraid of him. Granting him a hearing, that doubles as his arrest and sentencing, will show the kingdom that the king isn't afraid. And it will prove much to the houses."

Ana nodded thoughtfully. She wasn't completely blind to the constant low-level friction that existed between the five royal houses. After the king's injury, a small commotion had risen about his health and his ability to continue his rule. Of course, Ana was his heir, and her arranged wedding to an Alpha from another house was imminent. But that didn't stop them from pointlessly theorizing, discussing, and debating the issue, as they liked to do on a regular basis.

"Why do I have to be there?" Ana asked. "Is the whole court gathering? It doesn't seem smart for the entire royal court to meet this man. What if it's an attack of some sort?"

"He has been detained since he approached the palace and stated who he was. His weapons were taken from him and it appears he arrived alone. Tight security has been put in place all around the palace, and its grounds and scouts have secured the whole area, just in case his men are lurking." Milly's frown deepened. "I will admit his presence is strange, but I agree with His Majesty's decision to take advantage of this opportunity. That man has broken almost every law in our kingdom and has terrorized us all for years. An example must be made while we have him."

Ana nodded. That made sense. Thinking back to everything she'd read about him—Maddoc was infamous for his crimes—he was even more notorious for that fact that he hadn't been caught. It was as though he were a ghost. Not many people had seen his face, and sightings of him had dwindled over the last few years. He'd proven impossible to catch. If he could be dealt with now, it would give peace to many, and it wouldn't be terrible for her father either. Still, it didn't make her feel any better that he was even in the vicinity of the palace. "So that's why everyone was so… strange in the palace earlier."

"Yes. Almost every noble family and those from the royal houses have been affected by this man's actions. His unexpected arrival has many worried, and I cannot blame them. Some of the things he has done…." A shudder trembled along Milly's shoulders. "I'm sure most would prefer to see him dead and without the opportunity for an audience at all."

"Father must have considered that as an option."

"I'm sure he did," Milly said inclining her head. "I'm sure there is a reason why he is granting this man time."

Ana thought for a moment. "Will Mother be there?"

"All of the royal family will be there, Ana, as well as the royal houses, and maybe all of the noble families too. Many are curious about his presence, and I'm sure some will want to ensure he gets what he deserves. I wouldn't be surprised if he is executed straightaway in the assembly hall."

Ana nodded and took a deep breath, her stomach jittering at the thought.

"There is no need to worry," Milly said, her voice warm as her eyes finally softened. "It may be difficult to watch, but he deserves whatever comes to him, remember that. And he won't be able to do anything to hurt anyone, least of all you." Grasping Ana's hands and squeezing them, she smiled. "This will be a unique hearing—one that will be talked about for decades to come. It is a great opportunity to see justice done and this moment will strengthen you for your own reign. Try to enjoy it."

❖

Unsurprisingly, the assembly hall was overcrowded. At one end, opposite the entrance, a wide, fixed platform held the jewel-crusted royal thrones, while velvet-lined tiered seating along both sides of the hall's length provided seats for the royal houses and nobles. Other members of the court mixed in with commoners squashed in on the floor benches, which were always available for any who wanted to attend. Today was particularly popular. But for all the extra bodies, layers of nervous murmurings simmered in the space, replacing the usual lively commotion of court hearings.

Ana's seat was on the right side of the thrones in the small area where the king's immediate family were permitted to sit, and as she made her way there, she noted that every entrance was heavily guarded, which settled her nerves—somewhat. Maddoc wouldn't be able to escape.

As she sat down and fixed herself into the correct position, hands in her lap, back straight, and feet tucked under her chair, the king and queen entered.

The air sharpened as they strolled in, richly dressed in silks, jewelery, and matching maroon royal mantles. The golden crowns on their heads sparkled in the bright morning sun that streamed through the arched hall windows and cast a warming tint on the splendor of the couple.

Ana watched her parents closely for any sign of worry, stress, or fear, but the queen's smile was deep and genuine, and the king, although stoic, appeared relaxed. Their ease radiated out to everyone in attendance, and the murmurs petered out as her parents lowered to their thrones.

Ana loved seeing her father at court events.

It wasn't as though she rarely saw him otherwise— they dined together weekly—but seeing him holding court was an incredibly exciting experience.

Wide and tall, the king was imposing, able to silence a room by his presence alone. Ana enjoyed watching him create and enforce laws, debate with court officials and the royal houses, as well as deal with the accused. Each time he held court, he demonstrated why he was a great king, and it couldn't be denied by any other house, though they tried. She learned a lot about how he ran the kingdom, the choices he made, what procedures he upheld and why, but she knew her mother was his secret weapon. They discussed and debated everything privately, even though the queen rarely spoke at court. Ana had once asked her why she was happy for Father to get all the credit while she sat there and said nothing. Her mother explained that she didn't need to broadcast her involvement because everyone knew she was vital to the king—that was the importance of being an Omega. She said Ana would only truly understand when it was time to reign along with her Alpha, but in the meantime she needed to work hard at her studies. Ana found it fascinating to watch them. It all fed into her knowledge for when she became queen.

"Court is in session," a courtier called out. "Maddoc, a criminal with multiple counts against him, who has terrorized the Kingdom of Allandis for decades, is requesting to address the court, and more specifically King Orick. The offender's request has been granted by order of the king. All royal houses are in attendance; Goldfrost, Thorneshaw, Sterling, Redcrest, and Villemore. Prior to Maddoc being brought before the court, His Majesty will allow one query before the hearing begins. Are there any who wish to speak?"

"Yes." A nobleman, thickset with graying hair spouting from both his beard and scalp, rose from the far left-hand pew. "I have been asked to speak on behalf of the nobles." He cleared his throat. "Your Majesty, many of us want to know why you are allowing this criminal a chance to speak. He has committed heinous crimes, including murder, rape, arson, and treason. After twenty years of his reign of terror, we finally have him in our grasp. Why not kill him and be rid of him?"

The king paused for a moment before he replied, his voice relaxed and smooth. "There is no use in cutting off the head of a snake only for the body to squeeze you to death. Maddoc has gained support over the years. We need confirmation of those who've aligned with him and have enlisted in his fellowship of destruction. In addition, it is imperative we know how they are operating, how they get supplies in and out of the kingdom, how they coordinate and plan attacks, and most importantly, where they are based. This man can give us everything we need to eliminate his band of 'Mad Men.'"

The sound of snickering rose throughout the hall at the use of the frequent nickname given to Maddoc's men, but Ana was too nervous to be amused.

"Do we really need the information that desperately, Your Majesty?" the nobleman asked.

"We will find them all eventually. Better that the man is dead."

The king inclined his head. "We cannot underestimate the reaction of his men when news of his death circulates. It may inspire them to fight harder and longer to avenge him. And consider this, Maddoc came here of his own free will. His men must know he is here. I'm sure they cannot be so foolish that they're not expecting his demise."

"I doubt he is here to offer the information you seek, Your Majesty."

"Too bad for him," the king said gravely. "He has placed himself in our hands. There is no possible way for him to escape us now. We will get the information out of him, or he will suffer greatly before his execution."

The nobleman nodded and sat back down, a low hum rippling through the crowd.

Ana swallowed at her father's words, a hard ball of tension and nausea souring in her stomach. If his men knew he was here then they could be planning anything. It was all very well to mock and belittle them in front of the court—call them a band of mad men like they were incompetent fools—but Ana knew from her reading, and from talking to her father, that they were smart and dangerous and sophisticated enough to cause real damage.

"Bring him in," the king called.

Silence gripped the hall again as the doors creaked open. Heavy footsteps echoed across the space as a man entered and walked between the crowds seated on both sides.

A dark trembling gloom bloomed in Ana's stomach at the sight of him.

Huge and thick, he was a towering mass of muscle. A patchwork of mismatched grey, brown, and black clothing covered his bulky frame; heavy leather boots adorned his feet, and a ruby red cloak swayed from his shoulders while its hood covered his head and obscured his face. There could be no doubt he was an Alpha. He was larger than the guards who accompanied him, and he walked with a confidence not even the Alphas of the royal houses possessed. The arrogance saturating the way he held himself made Ana's stomach plummet—this was not going to be an easy exchange.

He took no notice of the audience on either side of him, his attention remaining on the thrones. When he reached the engraving of the royal crest etched into the floor, a few feet from the platform, he abruptly halted, then removed his hood.

Silence swallowed every last shuffle in the hall. Ana tried to drag her eyes away, to prevent herself from seeing the face of this monster who had been a malignant force against her kingdom for so long, but she couldn't. He held himself with the poise of a wild animal, waiting to strike its prey when the opportunity arose—deceptively relaxed, watchful, and predatory. He was unlike any other man she'd seen, and no one took their eyes off a creature so dangerous. Black, shaggy hair surrounded his head, and a short beard covered the lower half of his face. He had a strong nose and a gaze so piercing, it made Ana shudder.

"Maddoc." The king's authoritative voice cut through the tension. "You asked for an audience with me and you have it. Just know you will be charged here today, so I hope what you have come to say is worth it."

The Alpha remained still, almost statuesque. The solemn weight of his dark eyes captured the menace emanating from his whole being, and his gaze didn't waver from the king.

It were as if the entire court held a collective breath, and in that moment Ana sensed the aggression that stifled the room. It was so potent, it would only take one spark, one wrong word, to ignite the proceedings into chaos.

"You think I am that foolish?" the Alpha said finally. Deep and gritty, his rough voice cut straight into Ana, agitating the tremble that was already unnerving her. Surprisingly, his accent was untainted. Usually, the commoners, depending on region, held a slur or tonal dialect that made them difficult to understand, but it helped differentiate their location in Allandis. This Alpha's speech suggested he was educated—that hadn't been in anything she'd read.

"I don't pretend to understand the mind of a criminal," her father replied, his voice deepening as he leaned forward. "That does not interest me. All I know is your crimes cease today. I hope you have come with the intention of giving up your men."

"I've come with the intention to claim what I am owed," the outlaw growled. "And you will compensate me."

A hushed murmur rolled though the court, but King Orick did not move. "You are the one who has attempted to run this kingdom into the ground with your violent, senseless rebellion," he said, his voice hard. "You have failed. So instead of crawling into the Oakenshire to die, you come here to play the victim? That is your plan?" The king shook his head, disgusted. "You are more foolish that you are given credit for. Tell me the names of your men, or you will be sentenced immediately."

The Alpha didn't move. "My men are not at issue. The Royal Promise you owe me is."

The king stiffened in his chair, and Ana stiffened in hers. The Royal Promise was reserved for commoners who aided the kingdom in such an exceptional way that the royal family had a duty to reward them. It was detailed heavily in Allandis law. Milly had explained in one of Ana's lessons that since the inception of the Royal Promise over eighty years ago, unrest and dissatisfaction against the crown had dropped drastically. Commoners held the promise in high regard, seeing it as something they could be awarded if they proved their value to the kingdom. However, Ana was disappointed to learn that only one person in history had ever earned it.

"Why the fuck would you think *you* of all people would have claim to a promise?" The king's voice boomed across the hall.

Maddoc's head tilted slightly, his voice measured and deliberate. "I saved your life a month ago."

An icy horror breathed along Ana's upper arms. *No.*

"I killed the men who were about to murder you on your last hunt... and they would have succeeded.

Your guards were fucking ineffective and useless." His eyes bore into the king. "Much like they are now."

"You expect me to believe that?" the king snarled. "From a liar and a cheat?"

"It is easy to prove."

"Of course it is. You will manipulate the truth. It was probably your men who orchestrated the attack!"

The outlaw's eyes darkened even further. "I would never kill my own men."

"Don't pretend as though you have any honor," the king thundered. "Why you would save my life after all your attempts to end my reign? You are lying!"

"I'm not ready for you to die yet, Orick," Maddoc said sharply. "You will not die until everything has been stripped from you. Until all the riches you have amassed have been plundered, and the pain you have inflicted has turned back on you tenfold. You are not permitted to die until that has happened."

Ana had never seen her father so furious. He shot forward again in his chair, veins straining at his neck. "You may wish for that, but it will never come to pass. You have one more chance to give up your men before you are fucking executed."

The outlaw remained still. "So you will not honor the promise?"

The queen inched forward on her seat. "What proof do you have of your debt?" Her posture was relaxed, her face smooth and calm, but Ana recognized the slight twitch in her cheek that betrayed her mother's worry, and as Ana glanced around the silent hall, it was clear her mother wasn't the only one. Each body on every seat—from the houses to the commoners— leaned toward the throne, all eyes examining the exchange, even the guards had turned to watch. And all were silent.

Maddoc moved slowly. His hand lifted to his furs and dipped into a pocket at his chest, then pulled out a bloody, patterned rag that was torn and frayed. "Do you recall that I pressed this cloth against your wound? I tore it in half as your men arrived so you could maintain the pressure."

From the king's thunderous face, it was clear Maddoc wasn't lying.

Ana held her breath along with the rest of the court.

"You can examine my bow and arrows and my sword that you took from me when I arrived," the outlaw added. "They are unique. You will be able to identify that they are the weapons that killed the men."

"And how do we know they were not your men?" the queen asked, though her voice shook a little.

"Your people examined them, didn't they? You should already know they are not my men."

The queen shifted back in her chair, as regal as when she sat down, but Ana could see the slight drop of her shoulders. "Why would you save him?" she asked.

At that, the outlaw didn't answer.

"To be owed a promise," the king spit out. His face had deepened to a dark red and his knuckles were almost white as he squeezed the arm of the throne. If he had the opportunity to kill Maddoc from where he stood with his bare hands, Ana had no doubt he would do it. But the Royal Promise changed everything.

"Your cloth and weapons will be examined," he said stiffly, as though forcing the words out. "But given your lifelong mission to destroy me, I don't see why I should honor any promise to you."

A ripple of gasps and murmurs waved through the court, and prickles of dread attacked Ana's nerves. The refusal of a promise wouldn't put her father in a good light, even if it was to this man.

"If you choose not to honor a promise to the man who is the reason for every breath you take," Maddoc said darkly, "you will have a riot in your kingdom, and you know it."

"And you will no doubt encourage and incite it," the king snarled.

Maddoc didn't answer, but his wiry beard twitched slightly.

The king's jaw tightened. "And what is it you want as your repayment? What is so precious that you staged this farce? Riches? Gold? Is it land you're after? Perhaps a pardon for your sorry life?"

"All of those things are irrelevant and unnecessary," Maddoc growled. "There is only one thing of unmatched value that I want."

"What is it?"

"Your daughter. For three nights."

Two

The air in Ana's lungs turned thick. Her chest tightened and her breath hitched in her throat as she tried to make sense of the words she just heard.

"My... What the fuck did you say to me?" her father bellowed, rising to his feet.

Maddoc remained still. The guards watched him closely, tightening their fists on their weapons, but none of them moved.

"I will not negotiate my daughter," he bellowed again. "You will fucking die before you get in a room with her."

Ana gripped the arms of her chair, trying to find a way to take a breath. *Her?* What could he possibly want with her?

"Three nights," Maddoc repeated.

"Arrest him!" her father roared.

The royal guards moved in, but Maddoc still didn't move. His fierce gaze remained on the king, and the way he looked at him, Ana was sure he saw something about her father the rest of them couldn't see. She didn't like what it implied.

"What is worth more to you, Orick?" Maddoc finally said, his gritty voice quiet. "Your daughter's honor or your throne? If you renege on the promise, your reign is over. You know it. You can arrest me, you can blame me and my men for it. But it doesn't change the fact that you will be the king who denied a commoner, a man who saved your life, the Royal Promise."

At that, the court quietened again. Even the guards, who the king ordered to arrest him, stopped when they surrounded him, waiting for the king to reaffirm his instruction.

"I am not asking you to give up your kingdom, your wealth, or your reign. I'm not even asking you to give up your alliances or make use of them for my cause. Just three nights with your daughter." He paused. "You can understand that an Alpha has needs."

The heat that rushed to Ana's head made her dizzy. She lowered her head as her cheeks burned. So that was what he wanted. Of course. How foolish of her not to immediately think of it.

"You are a fucking savage," the queen said, her face contorted with disgust. It was the first time Ana heard her mother speak in such a way,

A dark leer entered his tone, even though his expression didn't change. "A savage keen on trying royal pussy, yes."

A murmur rippled through the hall again, and the queen wrinkled her nose as she turned away. A fresh rush of blazing embarrassment clawed up Ana's neck.

"That is not an appropriate request," the king thundered. "My daughter is not—"

"I don't give a fuck what you feel is appropriate," Maddoc interrupted, his voice rising above its low tone for the first time. "She is over twenty years old and well over the age of an adult, as set by Allandis law. In some parts of this kingdom, women her age are working, with six or seven children running around their feet while carrying the next. I assure you, your daughter is well-equipped to handle me for three nights—at least we shall see if she is."

Frantic desperation rose as Ana twisted her fingers around each other in her lap. Father had to find a way to get rid of him. It was not possible for her to spend any time with this man *at all*. Her father couldn't allow it. He just couldn't.

"I don't care about what is happening elsewhere in the kingdom," the king stormed. "We are discussing *my* daughter. She's not only royalty but an *Omega*, not some cheap whore you can rent by the half hour. She will not lay with you."

"Then you are refusing?"

In the silence that followed, Ana dared not to look anywhere else but at her father's face. Although he was usually impassive at court events, rage had twisted and reddened his face, making him more expressive than usual. His feelings were clear—he didn't want this man to have access to her, but when he did not immediately answer yes, Ana's heart began to pound.

"Good," the outlaw said, gruffly. "The repayment terms for your debt are three consecutive nights with the princess, dusk until dawn, in a room in the palace with an east facing window. I'm sure you have a room suitable."

With each word from his mouth, Ana's panic grew. Her gaze remained on her father, unable to believe that he hadn't outright refused.

"Tonight will be the first night. At dawn after the third night, your debt will be paid." As Maddoc turned, his dark eyes slid to Ana. At his intense gaze, goosebumps erupted over her skin and a nervous quiver skittered down her spine, but then within a moment, his back was to her as he made his way down the hall.

Although the guards continued to surround him, escorting him out, it was clear who was in control of the situation now.

Everyone remained in their seats after the outlaw exited, which was unusual for the court.

Ana wouldn't have been able to move, even if she wanted to. It was difficult to draw breath, and a persistent throbbing filled her ears. She rubbed her knuckles into her legs, her eyes on her father as she tried to calm herself. Father had to have some kind of plan.

"Explain why you didn't arrest him?" The same nobleman rose again, breaking the stunned silence that had fallen over the court. "You promised us he would be captured today."

"Did you not hear what just happened?" another man on the opposite side of the hall shot back. "He's owed the Royal Promise."

"So he says," the nobleman argued back. "Since when do we believe the word of a criminal and outlaw? He could have simply observed that incident. There is nothing to prove he was the one who helped the king."

"We will know shortly," the king said, his voice low. The troubled expression on his face fanned the concern in Ana's gut. "And it will be announced once confirmed. In the meantime, I want the hall cleared. Only the royal court must stay."

A low babble of noise increased as people rose from their seats. The royal court consisted of the extended household of the royal family as well as nobility connected to them and their advisers.

The commoners and the lesser nobles, who had attended the hearing, filtered out quickly, but those of the royal houses remained. Ana stayed in her seat, avoiding looking at anyone while the apprehension in her chest smoldered.

"You need to discuss this with the houses, not just your court, Your Majesty," Duke Milo of House Sterling said, as the hall cleared. "This is not just a ruling family matter. It affects all of us."

"Agreed," called Duke Aldous of House Redcrest.

Ana tried hard to not look over to where House Redcrest sat. The Alpha she was betrothed to, Duke Ryden, was no doubt in attendance, and although they usually tried to catch each other's eyes after court hearings, she couldn't bear to look at him right now.

The king held up his hand as the other houses called out their agreement. "I will discuss with my advisers first and then call for the royal assembly."

"No," Duke Aldous said, bluntly. "This is something we should all decide."

The king's expression soured further. "My daughter is not up for open discussion, Aldous."

"That isn't the only topic to be discussed, Your Majesty," Duke Milo interjected. "For example, how did you fail to mention that there was an unidentified man who aided you when you were attacked?"

"No. It is more important we discuss what will happen if Maddoc is indeed owed the promise." Duke Everard of House Goldfrost said. "And what the implications of that will be."

"The implications will be disastrous!" one of the dukes from House Redcrest called out. "If he is allowed what he wants, it will undermine the years of effort and careful planning that has gone into maintaining the royal line."

"Are you suggesting that he will impregnate her?" the king asked, his tone tense. "Because there are ways to prevent that."

"If he lays with her at all, it is an insult to royal line," Duke Aldous pointed out. "He's not just a criminal and a commoner, he is also a bastard. His tainted blood and seed should not go anywhere near the princess."

Ana forced herself not to wince at the man's words, but she was inclined to agree.

"Besides which," he continued, "she is an Omega. Our most precious dynamic. She must be protected from this obvious attempt to damage our ability to progress the royal line."

Yes, of course, that was also a concern. One of the expectations that weighed heavily on Ana was for her to uphold the reputation and traits of Omegas. Since Omegas were only ever born to royals, there weren't many who existed—most of the population consisted of Alphas and Betas. Even though she wasn't the only Omega in the kingdom, she was expected to set the standard in everything she did since her family was currently the ruling royalty. She'd met only two other Omegas born to two of the royal houses when they joined her lessons on the Omega dynamic. It had been nice to meet other girls her age who were also considered unique, but she hadn't seen them again. As Milly explained in her lessons after, neither of them were truly in her position, since she was the only Omega who was part of the ruling family. And that made her more important.

"Then we break the Royal Promise?" a woman said from the other side of the hall; it looked like she sat with House Villemore. "Is that what you're suggesting? Do you know what kind of problem that would cause for us?"

"Tell me," the king said, but the tone in his voice suggested he was well aware.

The woman rose to her feet. Ana tried to remember her name as she spoke—she had studied all the royal houses and members of the families within them, but this woman didn't speak often at court events. "The commoners do not think of Maddoc as we do," she began. "Some of them agree with his intentions, even if they don't agree with his actions. If they know he saved your life and you didn't honor the Royal Promise, it will destroy their belief in the crown."

"So we let him fuck his way around the royal family to appease them?" Aldous shot out sharply. "Is that what you are saying? Who will he ask for next? My daughter? Yours? The quee—"

"May I ask that my daughter be excused before we continue to discuss this any further," the queen said stiffly, rising to her feet.

Ana's face burned hotter at the various expressions that turned her way; pity, curiosity, indifference, muted glee… She rejected all of them. All she wanted to know was if her father was going to allow it. She stopped fidgeting and sat up straighter.

The duke nodded, his eyebrows raised as he looked at Ana "Of c-course, m-my apologies, Princess Ana."

Ana forced herself not to shrink into her chair and inclined her head. "No need to apologize, Aldous. I have no intention of leaving."

The queen shot her a look. "Ana, it is not appropriate for you to be here while we discuss—"

"My virginity?" she interrupted. "I am the only person here who is appropriate to discuss it, Your Majesty."

"Ana," her mother said sharply, the warning imbued in her tone and the flash of her eyes made Ana even more resolute to stay. But then the king spoke.

"Wait in your chambers, Ana," he rumbled. "You will be addressed separately."

Ana wanted to scream at him, to demand that he tell her she would not be given up, but the sudden tears that threatened clogged her throat. They were going to make this decision about her and she didn't even have a say. The injustice of it was too much, but she knew she wouldn't be able to speak without sobbing. So she pressed her lips together and rose, avoiding everyone's eyes as she made her way out of the hall.

THREE

Ana paced in her bedroom, waiting for her father to come and speak to her. Hours had passed but she hadn't undressed since the court assembly. Milly had arrived to assist her, but Ana sent her away. She'd tried hard to ignore the looks of pity she'd seen on her way back to her quarters—everyone was clearly talking about the hearing, and although Milly didn't act differently, she would have heard it all. It had been drilled into Ana that royalty didn't bow to scrutiny or pressure. The monarch had to be dependable and unflinching in times of distress. So she held her chin up and avoided as much eye contact as possible in the corridors, but in the privacy of her own quarters, she didn't want to pretend.

Her mind replayed everything said at the hearing, thinking through all possible arguments and options that would save her from the outlaw. She'd studied a wide range of topics, even the modern history of Allandis, and read almost every book in the royal library, which was the most extensive in the kingdom. Ana spent as much time there as she could, sometimes to research for her studies, other times, like this morning, it was for the pure pleasure of reading and getting lost in the excitement of adventures she'd never have. Surely she could think of something? But the more she tried to find a solution, the more frustrated she became. Clenching her fists, she swore loud and hard, and immediately felt better. Reluctantly, she began to nibble from the platter of food Milly had brought for her.

It was another hour before her door opened and her mother stepped through, still in her court wear. Although the queen was always composed, with an amenable smile, she wasn't able to hide the worry in her eyes this time.

"So Father is really going to let him have me?" Ana blurted out, her horror erupting.

"It's not like that, Ana." She spoke carefully. "There is more going on here."

"Like what?" Ana cried. "What is so important that I have to suffer him for three nights?"

"Calm down," her mother said sharply.

Ana clamped her mouth shut and forced the horror back down, her breathing heavy until she calmed.

"Where is Millicent?" her mother asked looking around. "You shouldn't be in here on your own with your thoughts."

Ana's mouth tightened. "I sent her away. I don't want to have to pretend to be all right about this in front of anyone."

The queen sighed. She sat down on Ana's bed and patted the space next to her. "There is nothing more important to your father than you, you must know that, Ana," she said softly as Ana sat down. "He suffers greatly at the thought of you being involved at all. But the Royal Promise is of great magnitude to the rest of the kingdom. It has never been broken, and cannot be twisted or modified to circumvent what a non-royal is owed. The Allandis people hold it in high regard because it is the only time where a royal is beholden to a commoner, even the ruling family, like us. If it is known that we broke that promise, it could have disastrous repercussions across the kingdom."

Ana swallowed, trying to stay calm. "And is it really applicable here?"

"The Royal Promise is awarded to anyone who saves the king's life. In this instance, there is no doubt that your father is alive because of the intervention received in the ambush. That was never a secret."

Ana clenched her jaw. It had clearly been a secret from her. "But was it really the outlaw? Could he be lying?"

"The men who attacked your father wore an insignia that is not formally recognized in this kingdom. It seems they may have been sent from outside Allandis to assassinate him," her mother said quietly. "But the examination of the outlaw's rag confirmed it was saturated with your father's blood, and it matches the other piece your father had with him when he was brought back to the palace."

Ana stared at her. "No," she whispered.

The queen's mouth twisted. "I don't want it to be true either. But it was pointed out after you left today that no one else has come to claim any reward for saving him these past four weeks. Your father thought the man had been one of his guards who'd died." She sighed. "It is unlikely that anyone would avoid claiming the Royal Promise."

"Then why did he wait so long?" Ana scowled.

"Probably so that your father would recover and be of sound mind to award him what he wanted."

Ana lowered her gaze, blinking as she tried to understand it all. "But the Royal Promise doesn't mean he can ask for whatever he wants, does it?"

"Normally, no. Only if the ruling king's life is saved, can the claimant ask for anything at all."

Ana squeezed her fists tight in her lap. "It's a stupid rule."

"It is. We have just been examining it for the last few hours, and it is very clear on this point. This is why the commoners like it so much, and why all ruling kings have very strict policies around protection and the training of their king's guard—to avoid a commoner having this kind of power."

"He's not just a commoner, Mother. He is an outlaw. Why can an *outlaw* be awarded such a powerful promise like that? It doesn't make sense."

"This law has been in place for a long time, Ana, with only one previous recipient. Outlaws like Maddoc didn't exist when it was passed—the ones that were around were considered redeemable. Including outlaws and criminals as part of the promise made the crown look lenient and accepting of those who may have stumbled upon a life of crime. I doubt anyone expected a criminal as notorious as Maddoc to exist, let alone do anything of such great benefit to the kingdom."

Ana exhaled harshly. "He could have killed Father."

"He could have," her mother agreed gently, taking her hand. "And that is one of the three things I want you to remember about having to deal with this situation. Your father could be dead now."

Relief and annoyance fought for dominance in Ana's chest. "What are the other two things?"

The queen was silent for a moment. "This situation goes beyond you, Ana. The houses will be disrupted by this. The ones who are aligned with us could withdraw their support and then we are at risk of losing our claim to rule."

"Why would they do that?"

"You are the key to a couple of the houses gaining more power. Being betrothed to Duke Ryden ties Redcrest more closely to the crown. Your children could also then be paired with potential children from House Thorneshaw. But if you are made to lay with this disgusting excuse for an Alpha..." She shook her head and then shrugged. "This has never happened before. Prince and princesses have taken lovers before their arranged marriages in the past, yes, but never something like this. You are the kingdom's most precious individual, and he is the noxious stain Allandis has to bear. There is no telling how the kingdom will respond. We are trying to see if this outrageous request can be carried out as privately and discreetly as possible within the palace, but as you are aware there were many people, including commoners, in the assembly hall today."

Ana's mind swam as she took in what her mother was saying. Ana and her future children had already been tied up in agreements with two of the other houses. She'd known of the allegiances, but not the extent of them, nor the damage to the crown if they were to fall through. "If we lose their support, what happens?"

Her mother patted the back of her hand. "Let's not worry about that right now, Ana. Let's focus on the third thing I want you to remember. Do you remember some of your lessons on being an Omega?"

Ana nodded. Her lessons about the different dynamics had been some of the most interesting and had led her to do further reading. Each dynamic had specific qualities that were consistent among them, which typically predisposed them for certain roles, such as Alphas tending to be stronger rulers, leaders, or soldiers.

"And you are aware of the sexual compatibility between Alphas and Omegas?"

Ana nodded again, resisting the urge to drag her eyes from her mother. This was not the time for bashfulness

Her mother's eyes were tortured as they gazed at her. "You must be mindful of any… reaction you have with this outlaw."

Ana inhaled sharply, closing her eyes for a moment. This was getting worse and worse. "I thought I would be compatible with Ryden," she said, opening her eyes. "I thought that's why our marriage was arranged."

"Yes, you are. But that doesn't mean you won't experience something with this man, Ana. He is an Alpha, after all."

Ana clenched her fists under her mother's hand. Arranged marriages were supposed to protect Omegas.

"You are not due for your heat, so that is good. We are looking into a way to prevent you from having any reaction to him at all—but it may be impossible... and unkind."

Ana frowned, but her mother continued. "The point is, you must not confuse any reaction as true feelings for this man. He is an outlaw and a criminal, and he has targeted you specifically to find a way to hurt your father."

"Mother, I won't forget. Arranged marriages are only for fated mates, aren't they? Like you and Father. How can anything that happens compare to what it will be with Ryden?"

"It can't." The queen nodded in agreement. "But it will be your first experience, Ana. You won't know what to expect."

Ana nodded. That was true—but at least she would have her time with Ryden to look forward to.

"Which is why it's so hard for Ryden," her mother added.

Ana's stomach dropped. "Do you know what he thinks of this?"

"As soon as you left, he spoke very passionately about this issue. He is furious. He's trying to find a way to stop you from having to go through with it, but he won't find one."

Ana was silent for a long moment, her heart sinking. Maddoc was trying to hurt her father, but he'd already had the chance to kill him and he didn't. "This hurts me the most, not Father," she mumbled.

"It hurts your father in multiple ways, Ana," the queen said. "The idea that his daughter would be subjected to the unwanted attentions of such a man is torturous for any father, but particularly that it's because he owes this man his life makes it especially distressing. It also hurts his reign and ability to remain king. You are the king's only child. Maddoc is trying to damage and end his reign by tainting you. If you are no longer a viable option to be his heir, your father should be succeeded by extended family. But in the history of the crown, the royal houses have never allowed a childless king to remain on the throne."

From what she remembered of her studies, that was true. A childless king had always been replaced with a royal from another house. "So I will be tainted by this?"

Her mother inclined her head. "Not necessarily. As I said, princes and princesses have taken lovers privately in the past, and many have lost their virginity to those lovers before their arranged marriage. Unfortunately this is not private and the man is a bastard outlaw, the lowest possible creature that exists in our society. But it's also not of your own doing, and you are still an Omega. So it's a matter of perception. Some of the houses will certainly argue it, regardless, because the potential for personal gain. But there are different ways to cast light on the same issue."

"And how do we do that?"

"Let me and your father worry about that, Ana," the queen said. "You just need to do everything we say, and tell us everything that happens." Her gaze drifting to the window, her expression mournful. "The one thing that has been established is that the outlaw is owed the promise. If there had been any way to deny him that, then none of this would matter. But that is the one definitive thing."

The queen drew her into her arms, squeezing her close. "Don't worry about it right now, Ana. There are still a few hours until dusk. Get some sleep and let us think about it. If any solution comes to us, we will stop it from happening, but even if we can't, we will protect you the best we can."

Ana awoke to a knock on the door.

She lay still, waiting for the person to go away—she'd already told her mother that she didn't want any visitors—but when the knock repeated, she padded to the door and cracked it open.

Duke Ryden from Redcrest stood outside. He inclined his head. "I apologize for the interruption, Princess Ana, but I could not let dusk arrive without speaking to you."

Ana tried to glance behind him for her guards, but it wasn't as though he was a small man. Large and wide with thick, curly black hair, bold, refined features, and the most beautiful blue eyes, Ana had always felt Ryden embodied everything an Alpha should be. "How did you—"

"Your mother permitted me to visit."

Ana nodded and let him in, discretely fixing her clothing and hair. Ryden was an established hunter and swordsman, and had well established himself in his dealings with the court, the king, and the commoners. He ensured that he made efforts to inflict change and was bold in making his presence known in political and royal matters. It was clear he was going to be a powerful political force in his own house, and it didn't hurt that he was also extremely good-looking. Even if they weren't fated mates, he was a smart choice as Ana's betrothed. However, today, he swept into her room with an agitation she hadn't seen in him before.

"Today's court hearing was a fucking disgrace," he growled. "They didn't kill that animal when they had the chance, and now they are trading away your virginity! None will fight for it."

Ana tried not to be affected by his words. "From my understanding, anything we do to prevent it will aid the destruction of the royal crown."

"If he takes you," Ryden said, his voice tight and his eyes blazing, "that will be the destruction of the royal crown. It will be the destruction of us all."

"What do you suggest?" Ana asked, annoyance creeping into her tone. Everyone kept saying this, but they were still willing to let it happen. It wasn't as though she asked for this. "How do you hope to prevent it?"

Ryden stepped toward her and took her hands in his own. They were warm, although slightly rough, and much larger than hers. "We have options," he said firmly. "We can leave. Pack our things and leave right now."

Ana's mouth dropped open. "Leave the palace? How will that help anything?"

"You will not be in his grasp, Ana." Ryden's brows lowered in annoyance, as though it was obvious. "He will not be able to touch you or use you to get to your father."

"If I run, he could chase me and kill me to get to Father instead."

"I won't allow that, Ana."

"Will you have a choice? How are we supposed to survive out there?" Ana said, pulling her hand from his and gesturing to the window. "He is experienced in navigating the kingdom—they say he lives in the wildest part of the Oakenshire, that he's survived the most hazardous environments across Allandis. How are you going to protect me from him out there?"

Ryden's face hardened, and Ana suddenly realized that she was insulting him. She tried to find a way to rephrase her point, but she couldn't. Because it was true. Ryden was a royal; he was not someone who lived in any kind of difficulty or who'd figured out how to survive undetected in the wilder regions of the kingdom, like this outlaw had. Running from the court was one thing, but running from that outlaw? It wasn't logical. And Ana would not ignore such an obvious difference in experience when her life and safety was in his hands.

"Anyway," she quickly added, uncomfortable with the way he was looking at her, "it will still cause problems for my father for not honoring the Royal Promise. The promise means he has to deliver what he says he will deliver. If I am not there, he's breaking it."

"I don't give a fuck about the Royal Promise," Ryden bellowed, making Ana jump. "It is stupid pandering like that that put us in this situation. There is no need for commoners to ever receive the promise of a king, in any circumstance. It should have been abolished years ago."

Ana gave him a faint smile. "Unfortunately, there isn't anything we can do about that now."

"It could still be abolished," Ryden ground out, clenching his fist in annoyance. "But no one in the court is willing to do it. They all feel it would be unwise to enact a new policy in light of this situation."

Ana nodded, sighing. She expected as much.

"There is one other thing we can do."

Ana shot him a quizzical look.

"I could bond with you," Ryden said, seriousness on his face. "Right now, I could bond with you and that may deter him."

Ana drew her lip between her teeth, worrying it as she thought. Bonding usually only took place at a wedding or during an Omega's heat. "Do you think it will take?"

"It can't hurt to try."

"Did you bring it up with the court?"

Ryden's jaw clenched. "I didn't see any reason to."

Ana glanced up at him. "I don't think being bonded will dissuade him." She knew it wouldn't—at all. The outlaw was only interested in one thing, and whether she was bonded or not, he would still have her.

Ryden thought for a long moment.

"And remember, you will feel everything that I feel when I am with him," Ana said slowly.

Ryden's nose wrinkled. Clearly he hadn't thought about that. "That would be…."

It was clear he found the idea repulsive, and Ana didn't really blame him. Who would want to be subjected to that?

Ryden exhaled a harsh breath and turned away, marching across the room before turning back, anger on his face. "This outlaw is taking everything from me, and I won't allow it! He is trying to ruin us, and ruin our chances for a successful reign by injecting himself between us."

"Mother said that his intention is to ruin father."

"Yes," Ryden said firmly. "And us." He moved closer to Ana. "I have waited a long time for you, Ana." He stroked her cheek, his eyes on hers, before slipping his hand to the back of her neck. "And now all that waiting has gone to waste. This bastard is going benefit from my restraint. I won't let him."

Ana stared at him, nerves rising in her stomach at the sudden change of his scent. "What are you talking about?"

Ryden's hand tightened at her neck and he pulled her toward him, crushing her lips with his. Ana instinctively pushed against him before relaxing slightly. Even though this felt wrong, he was still her betrothed.

"Ryden," she said against his lips. "You know this is not my choice, don't you?"

Ryden stilled, and after a moment lifted his lips from hers. "It never has been, Ana," he growled as he looked down on her. "If anyone is going to inflict this upon you, it should be me to do it first."

Ana froze, her breath cold in her lungs. "What do you mean?"

Ryden held her gaze for a long moment, then cursed. "I want you to remain pure and only for me."

Ana relaxed a little, smiling at him. "I will in my heart, Ryden. I am pleased that you don't want to break our betrothal because of this."

"Never," he said, his eyes burning into her. "I've been waiting for a long time to be able to call you my wife, and I'm still waiting for that day."

She jumped as a heavy knock fell on the door, and Ryden immediately let her go.

"Come in," she called, fixing her dress as Ryden inched back from her, his face smoothing over as he dropped his hands to his sides.

The door opened and the king strode through.

"Father!" At the sight of him, majestic and powerful, Ana's worries almost disappeared.

He paused at the sight of Ryden, a frown forming on his face. "I didn't realize you had a visitor, Ana."

She rushed to him and threw her arms around his neck, eager for his familiar feel and smell to chase away the discomfort and confusion that had dominated her since the court hearing.

"I was just wishing her well, Your Majesty," Ryden said from behind her. "This is an upsetting situation."

"I understand," the king said, his hand pressing into Ana's back as she hugged him. "So I will allow your presence in her private chambers just this once. It will not happen a second time."

An awkward pause filled the room for a breath. "Of course, Your Majesty," Ryden responded smoothly. "Ana, I will see you tomorrow, hopefully. I will be thinking of you hoping your heart remains with me."

Ana nodded an offered a small smile. "Of course, Ryden. Thank you for understanding."

As soon as he left, the king wrapped his arms around Ana and hugged her properly. "Ana," he said, his voice heavy. "I'm sorry I haven't visited you until now. I've been trying to find a way to stop this from happening."

Ana squeezed him tightly before pulling back. "Mother came to see me," she said quietly. "I know you can't."

Her father shook his head. "Not without severe damage to the crown or an uproar among the commoners."

"Surely maintaining the royal family is more important than the commoners being upset for a while?"

Her father led her farther into her room, and sat down, gesturing for her to sit opposite him. "That is not exactly true," he said. "The monarch rules and guides the kingdom, but if enough commoners are unhappy, they can disrupt the balance of society. That could be dangerous for us—the crown must survive at all costs, even if the current ruling family doesn't."

Ana frowned at the distinction. "So even if we as a family fall, there must still be a king and queen?"

Her father nodded. "That distinction is important, Ana. It signifies that even if we have to give up the rule, for any reason, the crown will survive. One of my brothers could be crowned or, more likely, one of the houses would be elected to stand, if their bloodline is pure enough, but the kingdom itself will remain relatively unscathed by this, and therefore the crown remains strong and in power."

"But how can the houses be satisfied with that kind of result?" Ana asked bewildered. "How can they be fine with your demise?"

"My demise is not necessarily bad for the rest of the houses," the king said carefully. "For years some of them have been looking to gain more power so they can command the throne. This is an opportunity for many."

Ana's stomach dropped. "So they are in agreement that this... man should have me for three nights?"

"No, they're not outright saying it, but some of them are not fighting as hard as I would expect them to," the king said, his jaw hard. "But, it makes no difference. We will not fall because of this."

"We won't?" Ana asked. For the first time since she saw Maddoc, hope kindled in her. "Everyone seems to think this is the worst thing that could happen to us."

"Ana," the king began. "There is always a way to gain an advantage. You will be in this man's presence for three nights. I very much doubt that he will be resistant to your beauty and your mild manner."

Ana flushed, surprised by the sudden compliment, but not missing the underlying message the king was saying. "You want me to get information from him?"

"If you can," the king said, watching her carefully. "You will be with him for three nights only—not the days. Which means you can tell us whatever you discover. If you are able to get anything to help us immobilize his men and prevent any further attacks by him on the kingdom, you will have made a significant contribution to his demise."

Ana nodded, but she doubted he would be so foolish. So far he'd proven he was smarter than most thought he was.

"It would be foolish to expect you to have the skill to extract information from a man like him without any training," the king added. "He won't simply offer the information. But just be observant and remember what you can. Ask questions when it feels appropriate, but do not do or say anything that will provoke him, Ana."

Ana inhaled slowly nodding again.

Her father's eyes drifted to the window as apprehension nudged across his face. "Maybe I should have let you take those combat training lessons you wanted to do when you were younger." He said it with a chuckle, but it didn't reach his eyes.

Ana placed her hand on his, knowing even that wouldn't have protected her. Maddoc was a huge Alpha with considerable skills he'd honed over the years. "What will happen after this is over?"

"He will be killed at dawn after the third night." Her father spoke so firmly, his tone sent a tremble along her spin. "He won't be able to get out of the palace. His life is over with this request, Ana. It will be worse for him than for any of us."

"Will it? I will still be tainted by this. I will have lost my purity and perhaps my ability to marry and successfully rule." It seemed like her father wasn't thinking about the consequences to her, and possibly being naïve about this, although she would never directly say it to him. But from everything she had observed of Allandis society, these "incidents" did not simply slide away unnoticed. It would sit with her for the rest of her reign.

"Not necessarily," he said. "We may be able to keep what is happening quiet from the commoners, but if not, there are ways you can use it to your advantage. Lets see what happens first. He may not touch you at all."

Ana snorted. "That is unlikely," she said dryly. "Not with what I've read about him."

"You studied his files?" the king said in surprise.

"A while ago, yes. He's mentioned in one of the topics I read when I was studying civil disobedience and society of Allandis. It's not particularly pleasant reading."

Her father nodded. "I know, but don't worry, Ana, there are ways we can handle this situation. Remember at all times what you are, who you are, and how you've been raised. Being with him for three nights does not change any of that—it will not change the history of your bloodline and the rights you have as a royal. Nothing he does will change that."

Ana nodded as the tension in her muscles finally dissipated. Her father was right, and that was what she had to make all efforts to remember, no matter what this Alpha did.

FOUR

The queen insisted Ana wear her full royal dress to meet the outlaw. She wanted him to be forced to remove every piece of clothing that signified Ana was royalty before he got to any part of her body, but the king didn't want to give him any jewelry or royal insignia that he could sell or use as proof that he'd been with the princess. So in the end, she was prepared in an elaborate, full-length dress, but not as formal or distinctive as what she would wear for royal events. Satin slippers adorned her feet and her red hair was neatly braided back into one long braid.

"Don't provoke him," Milly had said, fussing over her much more than normal. She prepared Ana on her own, with no handmaids assisting this time. "In fact, don't say anything to him at all. Let him talk if he wants to. Don't give him the satisfaction of hearing your voice." When she stepped back to assess her, tears glistened in her eyes. "I'm so sorry you're having to go through this, Ana," she whispered. "It's not right. No woman should have to go through this."

Ana smiled, her own tears threatening. "It is the burden of being princess, isn't it?" She tried to pull on the comfort of her father's words from earlier, but a coarse gloom had settled into her bones. And seated deep within it was an anger she struggled to control.

Over the past hour, she'd been prodded and examined by the royal medics, and given foul liquids to drink to protect her from disease and pregnancy. It had been one of the most uncomfortable situations in her life, yet she knew the worst was yet to come. Of all the circumstances of her life she'd felt helpless about, nothing compared to this. All that discipline she'd proved she had, all the time she spent showing her parents that she could be such a great asset to the royal family, none of that helped or protected her now. And that infuriated her more than she thought it would. This outlaw was using her to punish her father, and it didn't matter how good she'd been as a princess, it only mattered that she was his daughter. She'd been so close to some sort of freedom, under a month until her wedding, but now, and for the first time, she had no idea what the future would hold for her. And it was terrifying. Some small part of her felt liberated by it, because it meant she had some measure of control—what she did in that room with the outlaw would make a difference—but it wasn't the kind of control she wanted. It wasn't like the odds were in her favor to fight him off or to escape him. Even if she wanted to leave, like Ryden suggested, it would be detrimental to her father, and she couldn't do that. So even though she had some small measure of control, she was also more helpless than she'd ever been—and that made her furious.

Just before dusk, a group of the king's guard arrived at her room and surrounded her as they escorted her to the east side of the palace. The empty corridors, which were clearly arranged, created an eerie tension that heightened her apprehension. She gripped her favorite book to her chest, rubbing its worn, rough cover with her thumbs for comfort.

When they arrived, the guards spread out along the corridor and blocked each end. Ana stood outside the door for a moment, before taking a deep breath and opening it.

It was empty.

Exhaling with relief, she stepped inside. At least she would be able to familiarize herself with the room first. The guards remained at the door as she closed it behind her, and for the moment, she was alone.

It was a large, singular room, not unlike her bed chambers, except hers was attached to the royal living quarters. Her attention was immediately drawn to the enormous bed in the center. Tears and anger welled up in her, swift and vicious. Maddoc hadn't asked for that. He'd wanted a room, but he did *not* specifically ask for a bed. It was as though she was being offered to him on a platter. Bitterness stung the back of her throat, and she turned away pressing her lips together to avoid verbalizing it aloud.

A large window along the right-hand wall let in the last of the afternoon sun, and on the far left stood two tables ladened with bowls, plates, and platters of food accompanied by pitchers of mead and jugs of water. Heading over to the tables, she surveyed the spread—a large selection of cuisines from all over the kingdom. It was unlikely he would resist it, but she doubted it would distract him from what he came for. In the corner a small walled-off area contained a pump, basins, and a latrine.

Turning she crossed the room to the window and realized she was on the third or fourth floor. The royal grounds that surrounded the palace didn't extended out as far here as it did around the other sides of the palace. Beyond it lay the central city, the most impressive of the noble houses could be seen from here. Perhaps Maddoc asked for this room so he could escape into the city afterward. He'd have to go through the grounds first, though, and Ana didn't doubt that Father had his most accomplished archers watching the area.

She turned and paced the room, trying to settle her nerves. She surmised that the only way it could turn worse was if she didn't do what he said, or if she failed to keep her guard up in front of him. For the first time, she was glad that her father didn't keep her abreast of all the things that went on in the kingdom. There was nothing for him to torture out of her, nothing for him to use to damage the royal family, or her father—apart from her.

Finally, as the light in the sky shifted to a dim gleam, she moved to stand by the bed, set her book down on it, clasped her hands in front of her, placed her feet together, relaxed her posture, then simply waited.

It wasn't long until the door opened.

Tension sparked through the room as the outlaw stepped in, and Ana's hands dropped to her sides, her mouth dry as she stared. Seeing him at a distance in the assembly hall had not prepared her at all.

The man was huge—almost unnaturally large, like the giants in the old folk tales every child was told to fear. Ana almost expected the world would shake with each step he took. Thick, black hair swung just past his shoulders, and he wore the same furs and leathers he'd had on earlier. He was thick and bulky all over, and each time he moved something bulged.

The facial hair along his jaw and around his mouth didn't seem as scruffy or as abundant close up—it was as though he didn't bother to groom but still wanted his face to be recognizable. And what a face it was. Deep-set eyes framed by black lashes, thick, dark brows, and a straight, wide nose made him look not only rugged, but also powerful and somewhat mysterious. She'd read that he purposely hid his face because there was something horrifically wrong with him, which was why no one had seen it. She'd expected him to be as ugly as the trolls rumored to live in the swamps of the marshlands, but he wasn't. There was also no disfigurement to any part of him nor any affliction on his skin. The only striking thing about him that truly scared Ana was his eyes. Seeing them at a distance in the assembly hall did not prepare her for studying them close up. Pitch-black and drained of all emotion, they landed on her soon as he entered the room. It wasn't just their color—or lack of it. Within them was a harshness she'd never seen before—as if he'd never had a joyful thought in his life and his eyes could suck all joy from anything he looked at. Even though she knew the high society of Allandis had cruel and mean undertones, she'd never seen anything so dark and violent in their expressions. This man certainly reflected the concerns everyone had about him.

Thankfully, his eyes shifted from her to around the room, then as he fully entered the space he closed the door behind him, firmly locking it.

Ana opened her mouth, preparing to introduce herself, but he strode into the middle of the room, his eyes hitting her again, and the trembling darkness simmering in her stomach heightened.

"Come here."

With those low, gritty words, the tremble exploded into a nauseous cloud of unease. Ana stepped toward him, unable to drag her eyes from his face. He watched her with the same intensity that he had watched Father, but there was something different about it now, something she couldn't decipher.

When she reached within a couple of feet from him, she stopped and forced herself to bow her head. Maybe if she did what Milly said—didn't speak to him unless necessary, and made herself to be the submissive Omega that all Alphas wanted—then she could save herself some of the discomfort that was no doubt about to come.

"Kneel."

Ana's eyes shot back up at him, but his expression didn't change. Taking a deep breath, she slowly lowered to her knees, her dress puffing out around her. She kept her head down as he stepped forward, shuffling with his clothes.

"Open."

When she glanced up, she froze, her breath caught in her throat. The outlaw had unbuckled himself and released his cock. Hard, thick, and long, it swayed heavily, almost as though it had a significant weight of its own. Though she'd had lessons about sex and her heat, she'd never imagined what a cock might look like close-up when aroused—of course she'd read the more racier stories in the library, the ones Milly thought she didn't know about wedged between the boring land ownership laws and the thousands of recipes for pottage, but none of them described what a man's appendage looked like, only what he did with it. This Alpha's was huge—a thick, stiff rod that curved up slightly with a seeping bulbous tip, and veins scattering along it.

Her eyes widened as he came toward her, and she almost didn't register what he was expecting her to do until its warm, wet tip touched her lips. She stiffened, indignant that he was intending to treat her like a whore, but she already knew that was going to happen. She forced herself to calm, and let him rub himself on her lips. The skin was silkier than she thought it was going to be, and the scent that curled into her nose was nothing like she had experienced before. Deep and rich, it was pungent with strong spicy, briny, and caustic tones blended to create something so uniquely complex she couldn't decide if it was pleasing or not. She took a deep breath of it, and another. And then another.

"Open," he ordered again, irritation crackling through his tone.

Ana tentatively opened her mouth, but immediately he grabbed the back of her head and shoved himself in as far as it would go.

She immediately retched, but he held it in, the tip almost touching the back of her throat as she tried to accommodate it.

He said something, but she couldn't hear anything beyond her own choking. With her eyes tearing up, she grabbed his wrist that held her head down and scratched at it for him to release her.

Just when she thought she would certainly choke to death, he finally withdrew from the back of her throat but kept his cock in her mouth. Ana coughed around him, foaming bubbles of her saliva erupting from the corners of her mouth and dripping down to the floor in long, stringy strands.

"Suck."

Glancing up at his unchanged expression, Ana knew that he was not going to allow her to remove him from her mouth completely. So she sucked on him the best she could, her lips wet from her own spit and the bitterness from the back of her throat strong in her mouth. The taste of him echoed his complex scent, and she lowered her eyes to focus on that, trying to push aside thoughts of where his cock had been rumored to have been.

After a moment, he moved her head down on him, but before he got too far, pulled it back. He repeated this until it became a solid rhythm.

Ana tried to remember to breathe through her mouth but with him being so big, her primary concern was to make sure he didn't push in too far again.

Finally, after what seemed like forever, he withdrew and pulled Ana's head back, forcing her to look up at him.

His eyes remained intense and angry. "You haven't had cock in your mouth before."

Unsure if it was a question or a statement, Ana shook her head.

"Good," he said with a grunt. "You are lucky you haven't."

Ana frowned, trying to make sense of his words, but she couldn't think properly. He held her gaze for a moment longer before releasing her.

She bent forward, breathing hard and trying not to retch again as the tears that already filled her eyes spilled onto her cheeks. She angrily wiped them away. No. She refused to get upset. This was what she was here for, she had to remember that. It was for Father.

But the thoughts didn't reassure her as much as she hoped they would—there was still the rest of the night to go.

Firming her mind, she rose to her feet and returned to stand beside the bed, wiping her mouth as she watched the Alpha, trying to ignore the pungent taste on her tongue and calm the lingering terror of what was to come.

He stood over the tables of food on the other side of the room, and drew something out of his pocket. He cupped his hand so his palm faced upward and held his hand over each dish for a few moments before moving onto the next. When he had done the whole table, he pushed whatever was in his hand back into his pocket and began to eat.

For the next few minutes, he ate from almost every plate. Thick bread, stewed meats, herb cheese, honeyed nuts, and cakes, and other delicious dishes fit for a royal feast were all crammed into his mouth one after the other.

Ana watched him, fascination edging into her terror. She'd never seen anyone eat so readily with their hands, except the infants of commoners when she visited some of the villages, and certainly not with such strong focus. He ate as though it was the first meal he'd had for a while, or as if he wasn't planning to have another meal for at least a week. Perhaps it was both.

Finally, he wiped his mouth and turned, looking over the room again as he chewed the last of his mouthful. When his eyes hit her, she tensed.

"Undress."

Ana's cheeks warmed, but she couldn't look away. So much for trying to distract him with food. She swallowed, gripping her hands together tight. "I can't.... do it on my own."

The outlaw's eyes remained on her a moment longer, and then he moved to the walled-off area and she heard him washing his hands and face.

Ana closed her eyes and blew out a slow steady breath as quietly as she could, settling her nerves. She could to this.

The Alpha took his time washing, and when he finally returned, he stood in the middle of the room and shrugged off his outer furs. The expression on his face made her stomach jitter, but she forced herself to hold his gaze as he rolled up the sleeves of his tunic.

He came toward her and her breath hitched in her throat, but he stopped by the bed.

"What the fuck is this?" He picked up the book on the bed, turning it over and flicking through it.

Agitation nudged through her that he was touching it. "It's called a book."

His eyes darkened as they flicked to hers. "You brought a book?"

"It's one of my favorites," she said, hoping the shaking in her chest wasn't present in her voice.

A gruff sound came from his throat as he threw it back down on the bed. "You think I will allow you time to read it?"

Ana pressed her lips together as he rounded the bed but couldn't think of anything to say before he grabbed her by the arm and spun her around. Her dress jerked, and a harsh rip tore through the room as it suddenly loosened on her.

Ana gasped, pressing her hands to her body to hold the dress in place. "What are you doing?"

He spun her back around, gripping her by the base of her neck, his fingers entwined in her hair as his dark eyes captured hers. "Whatever the fuck I want, Analisa." The bass of his voice echoed in her chest. "That is why I am here." Before she could respond, he gripped her hard and dragged her to the window.

What she saw made her gasp. Under the darkening sky, a large crowd had gathered at the edge of the royal grounds. They were far enough away that she couldn't see their faces, but close enough that their bodies and clothing were distinct. They appeared to be commoners from the nearby fields, but why would they be gathered there? As soon as she appeared at the window, a flurry of activity jostled the crowd, some of them pointing directly at her and waving.

Mortified, Ana struggled to move away from the window, but the Alpha was too strong. He held her in place, forcing her to stay put. "Be still."

She froze at his instruction, breathing hard as she quietly panicked. Something about his voice affected her in a strange way. It was as though when he spoke the vibration burrowed deep within her chest and tugged at something wild and instinctive within her.

He grabbed her wrist and forced each arm down to her side, one by one, leaving her dress with no support. The neckline dropped to her shoulders, revealing her neck, and the Alpha lowered farther until his nose pressed into her shoulder.

The crowd slowly stilled, and although Ana couldn't see their faces, she could tell they were watching what was happening, and could see both her and the outlaw. She squeezed her eyes shut, embarrassment almost making her weak at the knees as the Alpha ran his nose along her collarbone and slowly up her neck. She exhaled and relaxed slightly as a tingling warmth rushed throughout her body.

He was scenting her. And the experience was... not unpleasant.

The tingle strengthened as it reached her nipples, hardening them almost painfully, and stretched along the length of her stomach to curl between her legs. Confusion swam in her mind for a moment, but it was chased away by the Alpha's breath on her ear.

"You smell better than I imagined you would."

Two rough fingers pressed against her shoulder, on her bare skin, and ran along the neckline of her dress to the center. A sharp pressure stung her earlobe, quickly replaced by a warm, wet sensation that rocketed the mellow tingle to a harsh beam of arousal that almost made her moan.

He sucked on her earlobe roughly, tracing his tongue along the edge. It wasn't until cold air swept along her stomach that she realized her dress had been pulled down.

Ana cried out, grabbing for it as it slid down her body, but the outlaw held her firmly at the neck and swiftly caught both wrists again, his tongue leisurely grazing her ear.

She whimpered as her dress and chemise fell down to the floor. The crowd was completely still now. Soon it would be too dark to see them at all, but with the lights from the room, they could see them in the window.

"I wonder if your pussy stinks like the cheapest whores in Allandis," the Alpha said, his voice low as his hand ran up her stomach to her breasts. "As the adored Omega princess, it would only be fitting if it reeked."

Ana closed her eyes, mortified as he chuckled. The man was a fucking savage indeed. She didn't doubt that he had somehow arranged for the crowd to be here with their focus on the window to see her at her most vulnerable. Where were her father's guards? How did no one from the palace know what was happening?

She whimpered again as he pinched her nipples and rolled them between his finger and thumb, before grabbing and kneading her roughly. She tried to remain separate from the feelings of her body— ignoring the sensations building up in her that she didn't recognize. It was all part of the false feelings her mother had warned her about. It didn't feel overwhelming—perhaps she could handle this better than her mother thought. What troubled her most was the crowd. She couldn't drag her eyes away from the mass of people still standing and looking up at the window. Anyone decent would move away, wouldn't they? They wouldn't stay and witness someone abusing her like this?

But even as the thought arrived, she knew that it was a ridiculous notion. Even members of high society and courtiers, did not shy away from seeking out scandal. And this was one of the biggest gossip topics of all. If Mother and Father wanted to keep this quiet, it was impossible now. Once the commoners knew about it, it would spread far and wide, across the kingdom, and even possibly neighboring kingdoms. In one moment, the outlaw had destroyed all chances of keeping this quiet. And he had planned it.

She gasped suddenly, a sting registered on her nipple. He'd slapped her! Before she could even figure out what to do he slapped her breasts again, and she was certain she heard faint gasps from the crowd.

"It jiggles just like any whore's," he bellowed out suddenly, causing her to stiffen. He reached for the other breast squeezing and tweaking it before slapping her again, all while shouting out to the crowd. "If you thought that an Omega would be different from any other female, I can confirm that there is nothing extraordinary about this woman, apart from her very obvious beauty. She is nearly of ruling age and yet has never sat on the council, never given her opinions on any policy or law, or contributed in any way that has positively affected our lives." His hand pressed over her stomach squeezing and pinching as he went, and as he spoke. "She is a pawn for her father, an empty vessel, a pretty shell he has hoarded to sell to someone else. Another man who will be the next king and will no doubt make all the decisions for us. She is lacking in even the basic common sense of anyone who would rule the kingdom effectively. She is only good for one thing."

With his final words, Ana finally came to her senses. *The bastard!* Pushing her arousal and mortification aside, she began to fight him, her annoyance building to rage. "You have no idea who I am or what I have learned," she hissed at him, trying to twist her wrists out of his hands. "Not all of us are criminals who spend our time stealing, breaking the law, and *fucking* everything we come across!"

She winced at the sharp tug at the base of her neck as he yanked her head to one side. It was difficult to look at him in such a position, but she could feel him watching her and she tried her hardest to levy her most baleful glare in his direction.

A rumble came from his throat, and it cause a spark throughout her body. "So the puppet speaks passionately." She didn't miss the mocking sarcasm heavy in his gritty tone. "And her choice of words are... interesting."

"Whatever you're here to do, just do it," she snapped. "Do you think this display will tarnish me any further than this entire agreement already has? Any more than having your disgusting cock shoved into my mouth?" The words came out of her so quickly and fervidly, she was shocked by them, but she tried not to let him see it.

"Things can always be made worse, Analisa." His voice vibrated close to her ear. "Always."

Ana's mouth tightened. At this point, she didn't care. The idea he was saying these things about her, about her father, had dulled some of numbing fear that had been paralyzing her. He couldn't be allowed to get away with making statements like that to the commoners. It was a bold attitude to have, considering the reason why she was there and her inability to truly do anything to stop him. Both her father and Milly had told her not to provoke him, but she was quickly losing any reason to care about what he might do her. In court Maddoc had been simple, if not somewhat straightforward, in his request. He wanted to debase the king's daughter by using her for three nights to seek whatever relief he was after. Based on the crowd before her, clearly it was more than that. He wanted to embarrass her as much as he could, tear her down, shred her reputation, and make her completely unfit for queen. Who would want to wed her now when everyone had seen her body?

So now, she was too angry to care about holding her tongue and being a "good" princess. Fuck it. Whatever he wanted to do to her, she would fight as hard as she could against him. She wouldn't make it easy. After all, his agreement was with her father, not her, and their agreement was to spend nights with her—but she didn't have to take it submissively.

"Then make it worse," she said, the taunt heavy in her tone, as she glared at him. The problem was, of course, he was significantly larger than her. Nothing she could do would be much of a fight for him.

The outlaw's head tilted, very slightly, something changing in his eyes

"You told my father I am of unmatched value to gold, riches, and even a pardon," she said hotly. "Now you're saying I'm worthless. Which is it?"

"You are worthless to rule the kingdom, yes. But not worthless to everyone. Your tight pussy is still worth fucking."

Ana was so furious she could form no words. She stared out of the window, at the crowd and tried to ignore him.

The crowd outside built steadily, until guards finally arrived. When they saw where the crowd was looking, they tried to do their best to disperse the commoners, but the outlaw simply chuckled. "Trying to drag a crowd from a naked woman is like trying to drag an alcoholic from his mead. The scandal is too great for them to care about the consequences. Especially when they are in a crowd."

"So you've done this before," Ana muttered, her disgust evident.

"It's not that hard to figure out how people will react." He grabbed her hips and pulled her against him tighter. "They are predictable. Just like you."

"I don't care if you think I'm stupid," Ana hissed. "I'd rather be that than a murderer and rapist. I heard you fuck animals as well." It was childish thing to launch at him, but it made her feel better.

The outlaw peered down at her. "Yes, I can see you'd be the type to enjoy folktales for children. Is that what the book is?"

Ana tried to glance at her book on the bed, but he held her too tightly. "That book is a great feat of modern storytelling, not a folktale."

"For you to even believe that an Alpha like me would need to fuck animals throws your intelligence into question, princess. You have an entire library at your disposal to learn about the world around you and the best you can do is believe idle gossip. Besides—" He lowered his mouth to her ear again. "—you just had my cock in your mouth. Did it taste like swine?

His deep laughter inflamed her anger even worse than his antics with the crowd.

"The library is my favorite place in the world," she snapped. "I've read almost every book and parchment in there. If you think any record of you is going to be favorable, you're deluded."

"I don't give a fuck what it says about me," he growled, suddenly serious. "But if you've truly read everything in there, you shouldn't be so blind about what's going on around you, and you might be able to guess why I'm doing this."

"I know why you're doing this." She glared at him, ignoring the fear that still lingered when his eyes landed on her. "And it's not going to work. My father will not fall because of this. The crown will not fall."

When he spoke again, his voice was low, deep, and strangely soft. "But you will."

Ana said nothing, still struggling against his hold. Then she heard horses. Nobles had arrived, slowing behind the crowd, their heads upturned to the window. Ana's cheeks burned. She closed her eyes, turning her head to the side, in an attempt to hide who she was, but it was very clear what was happening.

Based on what happened at court, they all knew what was taking place and with their fondness for gossip, it was no wonder they'd come to watch.

She breathed steadily, coming to terms with it. The skies were darkening rapidly and soon it would be too dark to see anything. But why should she be the one embarrassed? Her anger surged. "This man is a criminal," she shouted suddenly. "He is doing this against my will, forcing me to pay for my father's debt."

Maddoc's grip around her neck tightened, and he whipped her head back, his face hovering over her as she bent backward, and at the sight of those eyes, her fear returned.

"You want something to shout about?" he growled. "You want them to hear you screaming?"

Before she could respond, he lifted her upright and latched his mouth onto her nipple. At the same time, his fingers slipped between her legs.

Ana was unable to process overwhelming sensations that flooded her body. The hot suction of his mouth, his tongue grazing and flicking her nipple, was even more arousing than when he sucked her earlobe, and she couldn't hold in the moan that twisted from her throat. His large fingers echoed the action of his tongue, but worked a little softer on her folds, spreading her open and rubbing her so expertly, a sweet sensation blossomed, spreading up through her core and making her legs weak. As it steadily built, she slowly realized he no longer held her wrists. She tried to push him away, but one hand found his muscled arm, contracting slightly, and the other entwined in his hair, which was thick and luxurious between her fingers. Distracted by everything, and still held by his grip, all she could do was take and enjoy what he was giving her as the pleasure built.

As he pulled off her nipple and captured the other one, Ana caught sight of his eyes. The fury in them confused her for a moment before she remembered. He was not doing this to please her—he was trying to embarrass her. But even as she remembered that a crowd was watching, she couldn't stop the peak of pleasure that hit, flourishing swiftly over her. Her whole body tensed, and the power of her orgasm shook her as she rode the wave of sensation, humping her hips into his hand as she cried out. She couldn't breathe for a long moment, and her knees almost buckled as the feeling ebbed, her clit throbbing under his fingers as he released her nipple.

He rose until his mouth was almost on hers, his eyes looking down at her with that dark intensity. "I'm sure they had no problems hearing you, princess."

She glared at him as she tried to rein in her rapid breathing, but didn't have the energy to respond.

She couldn't decipher the expression in his eyes, but his scent was deepening into something too powerful for her to ignore. And it was highly arousing.

He yanked her backward, pulled on her neck to lead her backward until the back of her legs hit the bed. He pushed her down onto it on her back and then unbuckled himself again with one hand while he sucked her slick off the fingers of the other.

She turned her head away, refusing to look at him, but the scent of his arousal dominated the room, reaching into her nostrils and mouth to force her to recognize his presence. And more disturbingly, she could smell herself laced among his.

He lifted her slightly to shunt her farther back on the bed, and then lifted her legs and spread her open.

She couldn't help the whimper that escaped her, and she closed her legs immediately, but he gripped her thighs and pried them open again, the look in his eyes dangerous. "Keep them open."

Her legs trembled as she kept them in place, obscenely wide, and she tightened her mouth to hold in the screams contained in her sore throat ready to be launched at him. A trickle of hope emerged that he just wanted to look, but she knew that would not happen. She was ridiculously wet; she felt her own slick tickling her ass as it dripped down to the bed. Her clit was swollen and sensitive, and her scent was almost as potent as his. No Alpha would resist an Omega laid out to him in such a way, especially when her scent suggested she was aroused and ready for him. That was what infuriated her the most—her body betraying her, making it seem as if she *wanted* this animal all over her.

When Maddoc glanced down between her legs, he growled with an intensity that was so raw, it sparked through her body hardening her nipples to the point of agony and slick flowed from her. The look in his eyes was so incredibly vicious that the terror returned, bringing with it a thought that no one had mentioned. What if he was in a rut? Normally an Alpha's rut was inspired by an Omega's heat, but there were times recorded in the past when an Alpha could go into his wild and controlled breeding state simply from the scent of an Omega's arousal, and could cause much damage. If that happened here, he would tear her apart.

As he removed the rest of his clothes, she firmed her mind, trying to prepare for whatever was to come. She was doing this for father, and no matter if this Alpha was in his rut or not, there was some part of her, as an Omega, that would enjoy it—Mother had basically said so—she just needed to focus on that.

Maddoc dragged her to the edge of the bed, he grabbed her breasts again as he guided himself to her slit. Ana tensed, anticipating the impending pain, but for a moment there was nothing.

Then his hard, silky tip tapped against her sensitive clit and she twitched. He tapped again and again, watching her breasts jiggle as her body involuntarily jerked. His cock then trailed up and down her slowly, then in circles around her clit. A glow of pleasure spread through her and she relaxed as she welcomed it, but then his cock plunged without warning, stretching and dragging her skin as he forced her open in one sharp thrust, destroying her virginity.

Ana screamed and tried to clamp her legs closed again, but he slapped her thighs hard, making her jump and screech again.

"Stay open," he demanded, guttural and raspy.

"I'm trying to," she bit out, glaring at him even as tears formed in her eyes. "Wait, just wait a moment."

He grunted an answer and pushed in even deeper. She cried out, grabbing onto his arm and digging her nails in as hard as she could. Infuriated, she clawed his arm, and then reached up and slapped him as hard as she could. "I said w—"

He pulled out and slammed into her while she was in mid-sentence.

The pain wasn't as sharp this time, and even had a tinge of pleasure to it, but Ana was annoyed he was ignoring her like some insignificant gnat. She yelled and slapped him again, but his only response was to fuck her, slamming into her again and again until he'd built up a rhythm.

Ana was so angry, she ignored the jolts of her body and continued to fight him on principle. Somewhere between the second and third slap, she'd seen that his beard had slightly twisted into a *smile*. Her slaps had no effect whatsoever! The bastard was enjoying her outrage. But when his thrusts increased, she couldn't maintain her struggle, and that was when everything changed.

A scorching multitude of pleasure and pain overwhelmed her, assaulting every sense and every nerve. The brutality of his thick cock punching into her, reaching so deep inside her, spiraled an exquisite sensation all over her body. With each thrust it strengthened—sharp, raw, and magnificent, woven with a filthy eroticism that made her almost scream with delight. It was so sweet it became almost painful... or was that the other way around? Ana didn't care to figure it out. The more the Alpha thrust, the stronger it became, until she was seeking it, needing it, desperate for it above anything else. She writhed her hips for him, widened her legs as he slammed her into the bed.

The Alpha dropped over her, leaning on one elbow as he watched her, his hand still fondling her breasts, but Ana barely noticed. The position changed the way he felt inside her—rubbing new parts of her that made her shudder with pleasure. She ran her hands over his chest, appreciating the sight of his bunched muscles and the closeness of his beautiful skin.

When he lowered his hand to her hips and tilted them an inch, she was suddenly tilting on the edge of a precipice—weightless and breathless, falling helplessly into a thunderous chasm of pleasure.

Ana had no idea what happened in those next few savagely blissful moments, only that at some point the Alpha murmured, "Beautiful," in a deliciously gruff tone that made her stomach tingle.

When she came to her senses, the Alpha was lodged inside her, stretching her wide, their joining tight and painful. Of course, he'd knotted her. A whimper played on her lips, but she swallowed it. She couldn't process the thought right now; her body was already beginning to ache, and everything felt sticky and uncomfortable. Taking a deep breath, she exhaled to calm herself.

The Alpha moved, and although she had the urge to snarl at him to keep still, she was distracted by his nose brushing her neck again as he scented her. A beam of satisfaction burned so brightly that a vibration developed in her chest that echoed in the back of her throat.

The Alpha rumbled his approval and pressed his lips to the back of her ear. Tucking an arm underneath her, he lay his entire body weight on top of her, smothering her with his body and pressing his knot, the enlarged bulb at the base of his cock, deeper into her. Ana said nothing. Her purr vibrating between them coupled with the security of the Alpha's weight, settled her deeply. And it was so comforting, she drifted to sleep.

The Alpha didn't stop fucking her for the next few hours. Each time Ana woke from orgasmic exhaustion, disorientated and almost panicked by the pain in her body, particularly between her legs, he was inside her again within a few moments. The first time she had woken, blood had crusted on her inner thighs and dotted the bed sheets, but the Alpha didn't even allow her to process it. He flipped her over and sank into her with a low groan that made her keen. He pounded her from the back, pulling on her hair hard while his other hand tilted her pelvis so he could reach that sublime deepness that made her twitch.

He never listened to anything she said, content to let her wage her tiny war against his massive frame, which infuriated her beyond belief. She loved the way he maneuvered her however he wanted, squeezed and slammed and fondled, but hated that he ignored her, like she had no right to bother speaking. No matter how much she argued and fought with him, he simply did what he wanted.

And what he wanted was to fuck her in multiple positions; all over the bed, all of the floor, against the wall, against the door so the king's guard could hear, and even took her on the edge of the window, her naked torso leaning out as he slammed into her with his hand at her neck.

Ana did things she didn't know would feel so divine, things she didn't know she was capable of, like suck the head of his cock. She did it once when he was spurting over her breasts, curious how his pungent seed would taste on her tongue. A muffled growl came from the Alpha as her tongue dragged along the tip and then swirled around the shapely head. His semen swirled around her mouth, smearing her lips, and a surge of hunger peaked in her. The Alpha grabbed her hair, but she already had her mouth on the head, sucking and drinking his fluid as it poured into her mouth.

When he was finished, the Alpha grabbed her and yanked her up to his eye level, his dark eyes capturing hers. She stared at him confused.

"Why are you angry?" she breathed, her eyes wide as his seed dripped from her chin.

"I am not angry," he growled, but continued to stare with those heated eyes.

Ana narrowed her eyes. "So now you listen. Does releasing your semen help your ears to work?"

The Alpha's jaw clenched, and he swiftly lifted her up off the bed and carried her to the center of the room. Ana yelped as he flipped her over, placing her feet on the floor but holding her head down so her upper body hung forward. "I am listening, Analisa." He ran his hand along her spine, causing her to shiver. "I am listening to you scream and moan and cry out for me."

Ana scowled. "But anything else I say is irrelevant?"

"Not at all."

Anna gasped. His breath was blowing on her slit. "What are you doing!"

A rough grazing of her folds almost made her knees buckle. She peered between her legs to see the

Alpha kneeling behind her, his tongue lapping her pussy.

She tried to get up, but his hands gripping either side of her hips, didn't allow her to.

"Why are you—" She moaned as his tongue swirled around her clit.

"Your voice makes me hard," he growled, his mouth still on her. "So why would I want you to shut up?"

Ana glanced down to see evidence of that growing quickly as she tried to brace herself on the floor. Blood was rushing to her head and she was finding it difficult to think. When she saw her slick dripping onto the floor, she groaned in embarrassment but it was short-lived. The Alpha rose to his feet and slammed her onto his cock, lifting her feet off the ground and pummeling her like it was the first and last time he would ever fuck anyone.

Ana screeched, jumbled words pouring out of her mouth as she pushed her palms into the ground. His cock stretched her beautifully in this position, the friction sublime. She could feel the jolt of her ass cheeks each time he slammed in, and the way he grunted each time, she knew he watched them. And that sent a primal ecstasy careening around her body. As her climax approached the Alpha suddenly stopped.

"Did you want to talk about something, Analisa?" he growled.

Furious, she growled at him, shocking herself, then wriggled her hips to tell him exactly what she thought of that idea.

The Alpha's rough chuckle echoed in her ears as he drove back in and within moments, she climaxed, her legs tensing all the way down to her toes.

As her peak ebbed away, she went limp, disoriented from hanging upside down for so long, but it wasn't long before he violently dumped his seed in her with a magnificent, primal roar that made her whimper, then rammed in his knot.

In the moments in between their frenzied mating, while in that sleepy euphoria when he was locked to her so securely, the outlaw did little things to coax her to purr for him, actions that were almost tender—ran his lips along her shoulders, kissed her palms, scratched her scalp, nuzzled under her chin. And each time she did, he rewarded her with his solid, weight.

Ana didn't know how many hours had passed when she finally woke to stillness. She lay quiet for a moment trying to orientate herself once again. The Alpha's body pinned her down, his arm and leg draped over her as he slept, his breathing steady and calm. Ana swallowed, wincing at the rough dryness of her throat and mouth. Her body ached even as she lay still, as though her muscles had been shredded to pieces, and when she clenched, she almost cried out at the pain between her legs.

Her mood descended as she thought over everything that transpired between her and Maddoc. There was no doubt that Mother had been correct. She had reacted to the Alpha as an Omega, and reveled in the pleasure he forced her to feel. Most disappointingly, she had purred for him multiple times. According to her lessons, Omegas were only supposed to purr when in the height of satisfaction and comfort with their mates. Her body had indeed betrayed her in one of the worst ways, and the Alpha had taken advantage of it. She closed her eyes, disgust curdling in her stomach as she thought about the significance of finding comfort in the arms of a such a man. She was just as disgusting as him to find pleasure in the way he used her. Not to mention that she already had a man, an honorable Alpha, waiting for her, who she'd intended to do all those things with. Ryden was her fated mate; therefore, many pleasures or satisfactions should have been found with him, any purring she felt compelled to produce should have been for him.

Ana shook her head as tears slid out of the corner of her eye and onto the bed. She told Mother she would tell her everything that happened, but she couldn't. There was no way she could explain this. It wouldn't help them find anything out about Maddoc; it would only embarrass her. She hadn't even spent time trying to learn anything about him that could aid the king and kingdom. She'd failed.

After a few long moments, Ana slowly inched out from underneath his arm and leg, trying not to disturb him and avoid any unnecessary pain from moving too fast. When she finally climbed out of the bed, she headed straight to the table to gulp down some water. The cold liquid soothed her mind as well as cooled her body, and as she made her way back to the bed her emotions had settled and her mind felt clearer.

She stood by the bed staring at the Alpha. Looking at him now, she could see his appeal. He held many of the desired physical traits of an Alpha and she could see the attraction women might have to him, at the most crude and basic level. But that was no excuse for her behavior. She had lost her mind to the pleasure that he had forced on her, and although it was her first time, she had not even tried to restrain herself at any point. The shame instilled in her would be a stain on her opinion of herself forever.

She noticed the book she bought to the room on the floor by the bed and picked it up as she headed to the far-right corner of the room. Sliding down the wall, she curled herself up holding the book to her chest, forcing herself to remember who she was and why she was there. As Father had said, this Alpha couldn't change that. No matter what he did, he would not change who she was.

She remained curled in the corner as the light in the window brightened, and she desperately hoped that dawn would arrive before the Alpha woke.

Unfortunately, he stirred before that. She watched him as he grabbed the bed for her, and then lifted his head to look around the room.

When his eyes reached her, she forced herself not to look away, even though that annoying tremble in her stomach reappeared. She forced the feeling aside.

"Come here."

Ana gritted her teeth at the urge that surged through her to follow his instructions, and the swoop in her stomach at the sound of his voice. Why did Alphas have this kind of power over Omegas? It was unfair. Even her clit twinged in response. She dragged her eyes from him and focused on a spot on the floor in front of her.

"I said come here, Analisa," he demanded.

"It's nearly dawn."

"I have you until the sun breaks over the horizon," the Alpha said, his agitation clear.

"You've had me plenty of times," Ana murmured, her mouth tight with annoyance.

The Alpha grunted, the sound coarse. "Indeed. You have almost restored my faith in royalty."

Ana closed her eyes in disgust, trying to block out the amusement in his tone. "I'm glad to have helped," she murmured. "But at dawn I return to being a princess instead of your whore."

"I think you could easily transition to either job," the outlaw said. "You may have missed your true profession in life. You enjoy being fucked more than any whore I know."

"And you know many, do you?" Ana snapped before she had a chance to stop herself. "I forget that your reputation is littered with whoring and raping. Did my pussy stink strongly enough for you?"

The Alpha rolled onto his front, stretching the length of the bed as he looked at her in the corner. His beard was once again twisted in that annoying smile, and his eyes were relaxed. "I admit I was mistaken on that front. Your scent is delicious. But your insistence to believe in folktales about me is adorable. Particularly when you have been fabricated in the same way across the kingdom."

Ana eyed him. "What do you mean?"

"You are said to be the virginal, innocent princess." He raised an eyebrow. "You are nothing like any innocent woman I know."

"Everyone knows that I will not remain virginal and innocent forever," she shot at him. "In fact, my marriage takes place in less than a month's time. It's pretty obvious that I'm not going to remain a virgin after that night. All you have done is broken my virginity a little bit earlier, nothing more."

The Alpha's face darkened. "Your betrothed will not want you after tonight."

"He has really told me he will," Ana said "So whatever plans you have to ruin my life has already failed."

The Alpha rose from the bed swiftly, his face contorted. He was enormous as he loomed over her, and once again, the terror returned. Ana clung onto her book, forcing herself to remember that she was his prisoner, and he had already done the worst to her. Besides, dawn was approaching rapidly, there was only so much he could do.

"You can think whatever the fuck you like," the Alpha growled, his eyes blazing. "As long as you understand that you do *not* fuck anyone else until after our third night."

Ana shook her head, her mouth tight. "You don't control my days, only my nights. I can do whatever I want during my days." Father had said so.

"Is that what you think?" the Alpha roared.

Ana tensed at his sudden volume and pressed herself against the wall. Agony worked through her rigid body, but she couldn't relax in front of such anger.

The Alpha towered over her, his glorious muscles contracting as he leaned on the wall over her. "If you fuck anyone, if you even let anyone touch you, I will kill everyone who lives in the palace."

Ana glared up at him. "You think I believe you can do that?"

"I don't give a fuck what you think you know, princess. Do you think I don't have people in the palace? Guards and members of the assembly who are on my side, or working for me and don't even know it? Do you think if I didn't want everyone in the palace dead they would still be walking around with their painfully pitiful lives? You live in a make-believe world, Analisa. Nothing at the palace is as it seems, and you are readily able to swallow that reality because it suits you to ignore it. I thought you were some unintelligent puppet, no thought in your head to understand the obvious realities around her. But now I see you have just been sheltered from the truth and have no interest in bridging the gaps." He gestured to her book. "You clearly read, and yet you don't choose to read anything of importance, only folktales to make yourself feel more like a child when you are twenty-one years old."

"This is not a representation of everything I read," Ana bit out, jerking forward from the wall. "You think you know me because you have been in my presence for a few hours?" she spat.

Maddoc's brow raised. "I know more about you than you think. And I know more about what goes on in this stinking cesspit that is Allandis' high society and royal court. If anyone touches you, if you fuck anyone, *everyone* will be killed. Do you understand? From your father to your precious lady-in-waiting Milly."

A vicious hatred coursed through Ana making her incapable of responding. She glared at him as her fingers dug into the book at her chest. She wasn't exactly in the position to have sex with anyone else, she'd barely survived the night with him. But the fact that he thought he could order her around like he owned her, like she was his property, infuriated her beyond belief. He did not own her days!

"You better fucking respond," the Alpha boomed, his bitter aggression seeping into his scent. "Do you understand?"

"Yes," Ana said, forcing the word out as hard as she could.

"Good." The Alpha grabbed his cock and reached for her head. At some point during their exchange, he had hardened and Ana's eyes widened as he pulled her toward him, pushing her to her knees and forcing her head back.

She didn't have time to process what was happening or to prepare. He simply pushed himself in her mouth, and she opened like she was supposed to.

Ana remained stiff. Her position was awkward and uncomfortable, raised slightly from the floor by his hand yanking her up. Her thighs scream in pain but she was not going to give him the satisfaction of hearing her complain or whine about it. At least he wasn't pushing his cock to the back of her throat this time.

He worked in and out of her mouth, grunting as he looked down on her, and she felt her body responding to not only the silky feel and complex taste of him on her tongue, but the older souring scent of their sex that saturated them both.

He pumped faster when she flicked her eyes up to glance at him and soon, she was trying not to choke as he reached farther into her throat. Without warning, he pulled out and pumped himself with his fist as his seed shot out of him and directly onto her. She tried to turn her head, but he held it in place as his warm fluid splattered all over her face, hair, and neck, marking her.

When he finally let go, she slumped back to the wall, blinking back the tears in her eyes. He was reminding her of her whore status. And clearly she could only be a whore for him—at least until their third night.

He pried her book away from her hands and walked away to get dressed. Suddenly, the sun streamed into the window, and she breathed a sigh, grateful that the night was finally over.

The Alpha strode to the door holding her torn dress and her favorite book, and looked back at her. "Do not forget what I said, Analisa." The menace in his tone forced her to nod.

Finally, he turned and left.

Ana couldn't even enjoy the relief that flooded her because fear, anger, dread, and shame overwhelmed it. She lowered her head to her knees and cried.

FIVE

It was Milly who came to get her.

Ana wasn't sure how long she was in the room for. She sobbed until a tired emptiness overwhelmed her, draining her of all feeling. Having already realized it was impossible to leave the room with no clothes, and having been marked so completely with Maddoc's seed, sweat, and scent, she didn't have the energy to try to figure what to do.

When the door open and faint sniffing sounds came from the person tentatively stepping in, she hoped it was her mother.

"Ana!" Milly rushed to her and crouching down, grabbing her hands. "Are you all right, Ana?"

Ana lifted her head an inch to meet Millie's eyes. "No" was all she managed to get out before she broke into fresh sobs.

"Don't worry, Ana. You've already made it through one night." She squeezed Ana's hand. "Once we get you back to your room among your own things, in your own clothes, cleaned up and rested, you'll feel better and more like yourself."

Ana shook her head. She wasn't sure she'd ever feel the same again. Something felt broken—as if coming into contact with Maddoc had caused irreparable damage inside her. She hated him for the things he said, the things he did, and what he made her feel—both good and bad.

"Let me get you some clothes," Milly said, patting her hand.

When Milly returned, she carried a number of gowns and shawls for Ana to wear so she could return to her room, but none of them were suitable in Ana's opinion. She knew she looked like a disaster from the top of her head to the bottom of her feet. If she were to wear anything that exposed her hair, courtiers would notice she didn't look as pristine as she normally did, and they would talk. On the other hand, she couldn't exactly walk around with her head and face completely covered with shawls. That would be even worse.

"We have to do something," Milly said firmly. "Let's just go with a gown. Your father is clearing this wing of the palace—no one will be able to see you."

"The guards will see me."

Milly shrugged as though incredulous that she would say such a thing. "They are guards, Ana. They don't care about what you look like, only that you need to be protected."

"Don't be naïve, Milly!" Ana snapped. "Who do you think they talk to when they go home? What will they say? They *heard* me in here." Oncoming sobs hindered her ability to speak any further, but Milly was uncharacteristically silent. Ana had never snapped at her like that before, no matter what she thought in her mind, she never once said anything ungracious out loud. The bastard had already changed her by making her fight him so hard. "I'm sorry, Milly," she said. "I'm just… I don't want anyone to see me like this. I don't want Ryden to see me or hear about it, and I don't want Mother or Father to see me. It's bad enough that it happened—they don't have to see the result. And I don't want to talk to anyone either. As soon as I'm back to my room, I want to be left alone."

"That may not be possible," Milly said. "Both your parents are asking to speak to you as a matter of urgency to find out what happened."

"Well, they're not here, are they?" The words burst out of her mouth before she had a chance to think about it.

Milly's eyes narrowed. "I understand you're upset, young lady, but you will need to relearn how to hold your tongue. All of your training will *not* be undone in one night, if I can help it. You are tired, and it's causing you to act irrationally, but you'd better restrain yourself when you meet your parents."

Ana lowered her eyes. Maybe Milly was right. She sighed, allowing herself to settle back into that void of emptiness. She was too exhausted to maintain any real fight, and what was the point?

In the end, Milly collected a hat with a wide brim for Ana to wear over her messy, seed-clumped hair, and she paired it with a conservative evening gown that showed barely any skin. The result allowed only her face to be exposed.

After she was escorted back to her room, she sent Milly away—much to Milly's protesting—then took a long, hot bath. She scrubbed herself vigorously and lathered and rinsed her hair more times than she could count.

Afterward, she slid into bed, intending to sleep, but as she did a rough knock sounded against the door. She ignored it for as long as she could, but then a voice called through the door.

"Ana, you will open this door now." It was Father.

Ana took a breath. She couldn't exactly ignore him. Padding to the door, she opened it to find both her parents waiting outside.

"I am really tired, I need to get some—"

Her parents both swept into her room and surrounded her with a double hug. They'd never done that before. Ana rested her head on her mother's shoulder, taking comfort from both of them reassuring her and blinking away the flowing tears. And time slowed for an endless, comforting moment.

The queen pulled away first. "I know you want to sleep, Ana," she said, sitting down on the chair in the room. "And you will. But it is imperative that you tell us everything that happened first."

"Where is he?" Ana asked, suddenly realizing that she didn't know where Maddoc had gone once he'd left the room.

"Don't worry, Ana," the queen said quickly. "He's left the palace."

Ana stared at them in disbelief. "So he is permitted to leave and reenter whenever he pleases?"

The king ground his jaw, his anger clear, but then queen gestured for Ana to sit down. "We will explain everything, Ana. Let's talk first."

The king stood next to the queen while Ana sat on her bed. She tried not to move as though she was in pain but she was sure her father could tell.

"Nothing good happened," she muttered. "I didn't find out anything new, and I didn't... escape him."

She didn't miss the look her parents exchanged.

"Did he say anything about the situation?" the queen asked. "Anything at all?"

Ana thought back to her exchanges with him. "He said I should know why he is doing this. He told me I should know more than I do about the kingdom and that I am a fool."

The queen stiffened. "Anything else? Anything about the promise or about any plans he has for the kingdom? Anything about his men or where they are based?"

Ana shook her head again, annoyed this time. "We didn't exactly converse much, Mother. Why would he tell me that?"

"You are an Omega," the queen said pointedly. "He is an Alpha."

Ana stared at her confused. How did that explain anything? "There was nothing like that. He mocked me and then..." She shifted uncomfortably on the bed, averting her eyes. "... used me. Repeatedly." The mortification of having to say this to her parents nearly made her break down in sobs again, but she pushed it back sharply as something occurred to her. "There was a crowd on the edge of the royal grounds. I think he arranged it."

Her father's fists clenched and he exhaled. "Yes, we know. It wasn't discovered until it was already dark."

"How did it happen? I thought the grounds would be secure, especially there."

"There was a significant disturbance at another part of the grounds that drew the attention of many of the guards. There weren't enough remaining to disperse the crowd. We suspected he would do something, even organize two disruptions at the same time, but not that we would need such significant resources at both."

"We're sorry about that, Ana," the queen said, gently. "It won't happen again."

Ana nodded, but the outlaw's words floated back to her. *Do you think I don't have people in the palace?* She doubted it was true, but if he did, none of them were safe anyway.

"This is one of the reasons he can come and go as he pleases," the king added, his face dark. "The commoners are aware he has earned the Royal Promise and they enjoy seeing him enter and exit the castle."

"It's like a morbid fascination for them," the queen added, somewhat disgusted. "Seeing the kingdom's worst outlaw have access to the palace like that."

"It sends a terrible message to the people," the king growled.

The queen took his hand in her own and pressed it against her cheek, smiling up at him. The action calmed him immediately, and Ana couldn't help but smile.

"The wider kingdom doesn't yet know what he asked for as his payment," the queen said to Ana. "There are rumors circulating of the rewards he may be receiving—"

"Things he *should* have fucking asked for," the king thunderously interjected.

"—but it seems at the moment, nothing is dominating."

"But, how can that be?" Ana looked between them. "There were commoners and nobles in the assembly hall. There was the crowd at the window yesterday. How can no one be speaking of it?"

"The crown still has a lot of sway, Ana," her mother said. "And so do the houses. At the moment, we've been able to keep it quiet, especially as we haven't confirmed it, so among the commoners it is all just rumor and hearsay. With the palace allowing Maddoc to come and go, looking well fed and satisfied, it doesn't hurt us right now, as many think we are treating him with respect. Even that trick he orchestrated with the crowd yesterday, no one is certain it was you. The 'woman' they saw had your unusual rose-copper hair, yes, but she wasn't wearing a gown typical of your style. Besides which, it is too outrageous for the commoners to believe that something of that magnitude could truly happen."

Ana's eyebrows were so high she was in danger of straining a muscle in her forehead, and the relief pounding through her made her breath unsteady. "So no one knows yet?" Since this morning, she finally took a full and deep breath.

"Well, the houses know, since they were all in attendance and part of the discussions," her mother replied, evenly. "And the upper nobles."

"Oh." So all the important people. Her flood of relief was choked to a trickle. "Are you still going to kill him?"

The king didn't hesitate to answer. "It will look like an accident."

Ana took a breath unsure how she felt about it. Granted, she loathed the man, but she'd never met someone who had then been executed.

"What about food?" the king asked, interrupting her thoughts. "He ate the food, I assume?"

Ana nodded. "Yes, quite a bit of it, and drank the mead."

"Good." The king looked pleased

"Why is it good?" Ana asked evenly. "Why would you feed him and keep his strength up for what he plans to do with me again tonight?"

The king frowned, but the queen explained, "It's good for us if we know he will eat from us. It means we can take risks with the food we put in there. Perhaps poison him, or at least immobilize him."

They hadn't mentioned anything like that to her before. "What about me?" Ana asked. "Am I supposed eat poisoned food too?"

"Eat before you go in there," the king stated, firmly. "You shouldn't eat anything from the table."

"What if I have to drink water, Father? Sometimes I will need it."

A king's face hardened for a moment and then relaxed. "We won't do anything to the water. But don't touch anything else in there."

Ana nodded, but remembered when he was eating. "When he first went over to the table, he did something strange."

"Like what?" the king asked.

"He took something out of his pocket and held it over the food. He did it before he ate anything, and then he ate like he was starved."

"Did you see what he held?" the queen asked.

"No. It was something small that fit in the palm of his hand. He put it back into his pocket after—I didn't see what it was."

"Did you check his pockets."

Ana stared at her mother. "No."

"Did you have a chance to?"

Ana opened her mouth to say no, but remembered that she left the bed to drink water while he slept; she could have checked his pockets then.

"Oh Ana," her mother said, annoyed.

"Atara," the king murmured, placing a hand on the queen's shoulder to calm her. To Ana he said, "Next time see if you can catch a glimpse of what he used. It would really help us."

Ana nodded. "I will try, Father, but he is not an easy person to monitor. He does whatever he likes, and he is very... distracting. He doesn't leave me alone in there...." Her voice petered out. She couldn't say anything more, not to her parents. "It's difficult for me to talk about it."

Her mother's eyes softened. "You are safe now, Ana." She leaned forward to squeeze her hand. "I know it would have been difficult—we can talk about what you experienced later after you've rested so I can explain things to you or help you to understand."

"I'd prefer not to talk about it," Ana said. There was no benefit to her talking about her shame or being uncontrollably emotional in front of her parents. It was understood that overly emotional displays did not fit with the expectations they had of her, and she wasn't willing to disappoint just yet. With this situation, she couldn't ignore or bottle up her feelings completely, but she didn't want to be emotional in front of anyone, least of all them.

"I know, Ana," the queen said. "But later we will send in a medic to examine you and make sure you are healthy. You are not permitted to refuse him entry."

Ana said nothing. She just wanted to be left alone.

After a moment of silence both of them readied to leave.

"There are only two more nights, Ana," the king said, drawing her into another hug. "It won't last much longer."

Two nights felt like it would be an eternity, but there was no point in saying that to Father. It's not like he was the one who had to suffer it, so she just nodded and smiled. Both of them fussed over her a little more with words of encouragement, and then left.

It was impossible to sleep. Not only did it feel unnatural to be in bed while the sun streamed in through her window, but the more Ana tried, the more her time with Maddoc revolved in her mind. When Mother and Father questioned her, the memories had already started to blur together—she'd spent all that time after Maddoc left trying to force herself to forget them—yet when she lay down to sleep, her mind crammed them back into her awareness.

It was extremely likely that nothing Maddoc said during his time with her was true. He was known to be a liar and to manipulate situations to his benefit—exactly what he was doing now. But there was something about what he said that struck her. Something about the library.

As the hours passed, and the day stretched into midmorning, Ana knew she was not going to sleep.

Dressing in a simple gown, and fixing herself modestly, she headed to the royal library, surrounded by her guards and the extra king's guard that were part of her regular protection now.

One of the reasons she'd been reluctant to leave the library when Milly came to collect her the day before was because it was typically cleared for her to use privately for her studies. The king and queen preferred that she have complete privacy whenever she was in the library, since they knew she loved reading, but it wasn't always possible to clear the library for her and it only usually happened two or three times a month. This time she didn't care, she just wanted to sink into the familiarity of her favorite place in the palace.

When she arrived, her guards insisted on clearing the library for her, and did so swiftly. She headed to her favorite section—historic love stories—to search for some of her favorite reads.

For the next two hours, Ana read through some of her favorite stories; ones that gave her comfort, stories that reminded her that hope and love and sacrifice existed. After an hour or so, she felt much better, and even snoozed in the chair as exhaustion overwhelmed her. She didn't find another copy of her favorite book that Maddoc had taken, but she didn't expect to. From what she could recall, that was the only copy. She cursed inwardly that she had been silly enough to bring it to the room, since now it would always be a reminder of him.

As she was leaving, her mind wandered back to some of their exchanges. He seemed convinced that the library was filled with information or texts that would justify his behavior, particularly with regarding the Royal Promise. There was undoubtedly no truth to that, but he had dismissed her denial outright, simply because he believed she preferred children stories. Perhaps it would be good to prove him wrong, finally have something to say to him that would erase the stupid smirk on his face. At the thought of his quieter smiles, a reasonable level of anger surged through her, but she tried her hardest to push it away. He certainly knew how to enrage someone; he had enraged the entire high society of Allandis for decades, after all. It wasn't as though she was the first one. But trying to prove anything to him would simply mean she would be playing his game. And she wasn't going to give him the satisfaction of it. However there had to be a text in the library to help keep her from becoming emotional.

She searched out all books and files she could find that dealt with negotiation or interrogation. Of course there would be no circumstances that were similar to the one she was in, but there might be some techniques she could draw from. She took her time to read through them, trying to find some commonality with the scenarios presented. Mainly, the texts sited negotiations between farmers or landowners, nobles, and even sometimes with a Royal House. As she read on, the examples themselves became fascinating stories of their own.

"I am surprised to see you studying."

Ana looked up to see her mother approaching the table where she sat.

"I thought you were going to try to get some sleep?" she said, smiling as she slid into the chair next to Ana.

"I tried. But I couldn't."

"And you thought studying might help you get there," her mother chuckled. "I can see your reasoning."

Ana smiled with her. "I thought maybe I could find some way to deal with the outlaw so I didn't get so..."

Her mother watched carefully as you try to search the word. "Sad?" she suggested. "Tearful? Depressed?"

"Angry," Ana completed.

"Angry?" The queen shot her strange look. "What did he say to make you angry?"

"Just the things I told you—that I'm stupid and I don't know anything that's going on around me..."

"You know that he is a manipulator," the queen said. "If he is angering you, it's because that is his intention."

"I know," Ana said. "I'm trying to find a way to be more emotionless tonight."

The queen nodded thoughtfully. "I'm not sure you'll find anything in this library, Ana. Not many studies have been done about the emotional connection between Alphas and Omegas."

That was surprising. "Why not?"

"Mostly because royal couples tend to be extremely sensitive about their privacy. Usually, we talk to each other so that we know what to expect." She tilted her head as she held Ana's gaze. "It is really my duty to discuss with you what to expect with your bonded Alpha. This is a tricky situation, because he's not that, but you can still ask me whatever you want to know."

Ana fidgeted with the corner of a piece of parchment as she thought for a long moment. "You said before that I might have false feelings?"

The queen inclined her head. "Not false as such, but they may lead you to think that you are more connected to this man than you are. As Omegas our feelings are very overwhelming when we are with an Alpha sexually."

"Does that happen for every Omega? Did that happen with you and father?"

"It happens to some degree between all Alphas and Omegas," the queen explained. "But sometimes it is more extreme. As you well know, arranged marriages are between fated mates, which your father and I are. Even if we weren't royalty, we would be compatible."

"And it's the same with me and Ryden?"

"Absolutely," her mother said firmly. "Arranged marriages are planned and decided through an extensive amount of consideration and research. Ryden wouldn't have been chosen if he wasn't the perfect Alpha male for you."

"And there's no mistake about that?" Ana asked, thinking about the many times she purred for the outlaw.

"No." Her mother was resolute. "Mistakes might be made if we're talking about the whole population of

Allandis, or commoners who don't have access to our scholars who study this kind of thing. But it's never wrong for royalty."

"Then what I will experience with Ryden will be better."

The queen smiled and her body seemed to relax. "I can guarantee it will be," she confirmed. "You know that you at least have that to look forward to. It's a reason to push through tonight and tomorrow night."

A weight lifted off Ana's chest. Her compulsion to purr must have been because she was having sex for the first time. That was all it probably was. "Why did you make a point earlier about him being an Alpha and me being an Omega? What did you mean?"

The queen leaned forward on the table. "The connection between Alpha and Omega can potentially be very strong once both submit to it. You may feel you are at the mercy of your body with him, but in some respects, so is he. You could have used that to your advantage, but…." She offered a soft smile. "It was unfair of me to expect you to know that."

"I don't know how I would do that anyway," Ana said. "He was completely in control the whole time."

"Probably because he is more sexually experienced. But now you have experienced being with him, you can try to exert your own will on him, and yourself."

Ana frowned at her mother. "In what way?"

"Start with something small. Like, this evening commit yourself to withholding two things only, things that you readily did last night that you don't want to do again. If you succeed, then you know that by tomorrow night you will be ready to try something else, hopefully something that will force him to reveal something to you that he never planned to."

"What if he's angry about it?"

Mother inclined her head. "That is where it becomes tricky and dangerous, Ana. I don't want you to provoke him more than necessary, but if you choose two things he didn't ask you to do, then he either won't notice or care, or he will tell you to do it, in which case that puts you in the position of power. In any case, it will be good discipline for you."

That seemed like something she could try, and better than what she'd been hoping to find in the documents about negotiation. Of course, Maddoc probably couldn't really be negotiated with, but she needed techniques and methods to try for herself—to stop herself from being so affected by him.

"And you have to stop thinking of him like some entity that is magical or special," the queen added. "He is a man. He may be somewhat different to other men in a lot of ways, more base and animalistic, but he is still just a man. Once you force yourself to see that, it will help you to be able to think clearer when you're in his presence."

Ana smiled. That was exactly what she needed to hear. "That will definitely help, Mother. Thank you."

"You are very welcome, my beautiful daughter," the queen said smiling. She leaned forward and drew Ana into another hug. "You are, of course, welcome to stay here as long as you wish, but you should really try to get some sleep so you are not too tired to make your best efforts tonight."

Ana nodded. She wasn't sure there was much she could learn from what she was reading. As fascinating as it was, it wasn't helping her. Mother's suggestion was much better.

After her mother left, she returned all of the books and files and collected everything she could find about Maddoc. She'd read them all before, but that was when she was viewing him as a faceless grandiose menace she'd never seen or met. But Mother was right—he was just a man. Rereading the documents with that in mind might help her do what Mother suggested. She desperately wanted to stop purring for him. It implied certain things she wasn't comfortable with and threw everything into question with Ryden. That would be the first thing she would try her hardest to withhold. She needed to figure out what the second thing would be, but for the first time, since he had entered the assembly hall, she was truly hopeful she could survive him.

Six

Thankfully she slept well when she went back her to bed chambers, even if only for a short time.

The medic woke her for her examination, which was painful this time. Apart from drinking the disgusting liquids again, he had her spread her legs so he could assess any "damage." Fortunately, he had some balms that helped soothe her, but then he spent way too long advising her to ensure she was well lubricated tonight. Ana was sure the old man was enjoying seeing her turn every shade of red possible.

She then spent the next couple of hours reading over the material regarding Maddoc. Halfway through, Milly brought her a meal, and she, of course, couldn't help fussing over her—if she'd eaten enough, drank enough, if her clothes were right—and generally getting in the way of her reading.

"Has all of high society heard about what happened in court yesterday?" she said abruptly, interrupting Milly midsentence. Usually Milly refused to discuss what she called "news for idle tongues and minds," but Ana was curious to know if she would this time.

Milly fell silent. "It is all anyone is talking about," she admitted finally, her stiff tone heavy with disapproval. "I've stayed away from discussions about it. I see no need to talk about it, and I expressed that opinion clearly and violently to anyone who dares raise it in my presence."

Ana nodded, a smile playing on her lips. Protective, second-mother Milly was clearly upset and insulted by the gossip. "You suggested I shouldn't talk to him at all."

Milly dipped her head in a sharp nod. "I did. I know your parents have their well-meaning agenda, but I don't think it is ever wise for an Omega to provoke an Alpha. If you've angered him, he has two more nights to make you suffer for it. And this particular Alpha is very dangerous."

Ana tilted her head as she gazed at her. Milly had been the one to deliver almost all of her lessons on a variety of topics. "Why do you think he is doing this? Saving Father for a promise and then demanding me?"

Milly shook her head slowly, her blue eyes troubled. "I'm not sure, Ana. But he is not as stupid as court the allows everyone to believe. He doesn't act as randomly or as foolishly as people think. He has always demonstrated a careful approach to almost everything he does and uses specific strategies to make sure maximum damaged is caused when he wants it to be."

Ana's mouth went dry. "So you think there is a grander reason for this? Other than him just wanting to lay with me."

"Undoubtedly," Milly said, lowering her voice to a murmur. "But it's not for me to speculate, particularly to you. Your parents have been very clear about it. I find myself at odds with them for the first time, because I just want you to survive this. I don't care about anything else. I know they must also be concerned about wider issues that I have no right to ignore."

Ana met her gaze, unease creeping into her. What could Maddoc possibly be planning? The end of the crown? That seemed to be what her parents were mostly concerned about preventing, but how would he accomplish that? Currently he was only protected by the promise, and Father already planned to kill him at dawn after the last night.

Maddoc had hinted that she could figure it out if she bothered to read, but reading was the main activity she'd partaken in her whole life. She'd seen nothing that could explain this. "How do you know about his strategies?"

"It's in all the material about him. I studied them, read between the lines, and saw patterns and similarities that arose."

Ana's frown deepened. Milly had never spoken about analyzing text in that way before. Maybe that was how she taught Ana her lessons.

"But that's nothing you have to worry about, Ana," Milly added, hastily. "Just do what your parents have asked. But stay safe."

❖

Ana spent the rest of the afternoon studying Maddoc's recorded movements in the kingdom. Milly was right—he was indeed very clever. He used disruptions on one side of a village or town as a distraction to rob a building on the other side, similar to what he did with the crowd last night. Or he created some kind of diversion to cause an entire noble family to leave their house so he could rob them twice—their household, and while they were on the road. It seemed he managed to have plans for each of the buildings he targeted because no one ever saw him when he entered, indicating he knew the staff's routines. Everything about the way he operated suggested he had intimate knowledge of the upper nobility and potentially the royal houses too. He had never directly attacked the palace, so there was no way of knowing how acquainted he was with it or with the ruling family, but he clearly knew the rumors about Ana.

By the time dusk was approaching, Ana had built a more accurate picture of him. And regardless of what Mother said, it was somewhat frightening.

The man was a heinous criminal. His reputation preceded him, as an exceptional archer and swordsman who'd kill anyone who got in his way, or anyone who'd seen his face, which was why no one knew what he looked like. His victims included women and children of both royal and common blood. He burned down villages and towns to steal gold and other precious items held in their treasuries, and his men used the destruction to rape women and steal boys of fifteen and up who would become part of their "fellowship," twisting their minds by promising them riches and women.

It was reported that he had thousands of men in his guild—not all of them were known, and some hid in plain sight as men of respectable stature. Apart from the children, he also recruited from those made nameless from failing to pay taxes on their land or those who were outright criminals. Most of the men wore masks when taking part in his criminal activities, but some of them didn't. As such, there were a number of sketches in the files, but never a sketch of the man himself. It was suggested in one document that he had spies in either the royal assembly or the royal court, which made him a powerful threat. But the notion had been discarded after further analysis.

Ana tried to objectively analyze what she read, but it was difficult. Maddoc was the most destructive man in Allandis, and what stood out to her the most was his utter lack of concern for civilized life. He didn't care who he hurt in his crusade. Everything he did was for his own gain, and he took pleasure in hurting innocent commoners in the process. It was sickening, and she detested that she'd had him inside her.

She remained confused about his approach to the Royal Promise; it didn't make sense he used it for sex with her when he could have taken more direct steps to tear down the kingdom. He could have acquired much with that promise; a pardon, land, gold, anything of significant value to the traditions and history of the royals. Something wasn't right about his request for her, but she couldn't figure it out.

Thoughts whirled in her mind as she prepared for dusk, bathing and braiding her hair, and dressing in another elaborate gown.

By the time the guards collected her, she had decided on the second thing she would withhold; her anger. Maddoc was the only person who had managed to somehow burrow down deep into her being, skipping all of her careful training, and made her react instinctively, even sometimes causing her to bypass sensible thinking. It had to be because he was an Alpha. She didn't like it. Maybe that was his plan?

One thing Maddoc had been right about was that she wasn't a child anymore, and she needed to act like it. Although the legal age of adulthood in Allandis was eighteen, many didn't assert themselves as adults until twenty-two. Ridiculous as it was, Allandis mythology had always revered double numbers, and twenty-two was when most people married, bought land, and embraced life as an adult. Ana was twenty-two in three weeks—the day before her wedding, but she wasn't a child. She should be doing whatever she could in this situation to help not only her parents, but the kingdom as well. It was her duty.

So as she walked down the empty corridors of the palace, she affirmed her decisions; no purring, no emotional responses. Even if she couldn't find out what Maddoc planned, he would no longer be using her as his puppet.

The room looked the same. An elaborate array of food was laid out on the tables, just like before, and the bed had been remade as though nothing had happened. Even the hint of their scents had permeated the room was so faint it was like a lingering memory of something that had once been powerful.

Ana went to the window. This time, multiple guards strode across the grounds and many were positioned along the edge to move along anyone who loitered. At least some steps were being taken to minimize another crowd. But it wasn't likely Maddoc would try the same thing twice.

She positioned herself next to the bed, on the right-hand side of the room nearby the window, where she had stood before, reaffirming to herself the decisions she made for tonight.

She was surprised when the door opened within a few moments. Maddoc stepped in, looking as huge as he did the previous night. An air of menace surrounded his large frame and the joyless gaze he had entered the room with yesterday was back, although Ana couldn't recall seeing it when he'd left that morning. He wore a mix of slightly different furs, but mostly everything was the same. He stepped in, locked the door behind him, and walked to the middle of the room as he had done the previous night.

Ana glanced at the window again, pushing her surprise away. "You're early."

Maddoc didn't respond, simply staring at her with an intensity that made goosebumps rush up the back of her arms and spark that annoying tremble that lived in her stomach that began yesterday when she first saw him.

She shifted her feet, waiting for him to say or do something, but when she glanced at the window she suddenly realized it wasn't yet dusk. He couldn't touch her until the sun had set. He was waiting.

For some reason, that made her more nervous. Why had he come early only to stand there and wait?

Maybe he was trying to intimidate her. Exhaling a breath, she pushed the discomfort aside.

They stood facing each other, waiting for dusk to arrive.

Ana took the opportunity to examine him more closely. Strangely, although he was certainly rough and rugged at first glance, he clearly took efforts to maintain elements of his appearance. His boots, while dusty, were well made and had no holes or scuffs. His clothes were not frayed or torn, and his hair was not matted with dirt. In fact, today, he had the top part pulled back away from his face, giving him a more civilized appearance than yesterday. He might not groom, but he wasn't disheveled. He also didn't look like someone made wealthy by robbing multiple towns and villages. She eyed his clothing, wondered what he was doing with his riches, and why he didn't already have a wife. The files on him included multiple rumors about him, which even the authors made clear were not based on any real evidence. One rumor claimed he'd had a wife who had been executed by the royal assembly, another claimed it was his sister, another asserted he was a sexual deviant who could only find release and comfort with animals, another said he and his men lived with a group of whores whom they all rotated through.

Ana was inclined to believe the last one, and that made her feel... strange. Her eyes dragged up Maddoc's chest, and the tremble in her stomach strengthened to a fluttering of desire as she remembered his massive torso on top of her, contracting beautifully as he thrust.

Ana caught the thought, shocked with herself. Flicking her eyes up to look at Maddoc, she hoped her desire hadn't been obvious, even though her face was warm. However, Maddoc was still looking at her with that brutal gaze—he hadn't deviated and hadn't moved.

Ana swallowed, turned her attention to other areas of the room, before returning to him, realizing something. He held a book in his hands.

"You brought my book back?" she asked tentatively.

Surprisingly, he answered. "No."

She peered at his hands. "What is it, then?"

"A different book. One that is actually worth reading."

Ana's eyes narrowed. "The book you stole from me is one of the best stories that exists."

"Untrue. It has no fucking in it."

Ana flushed and averted her eyes. "That is n-not the standard for a good book." Her eyes snapped back to him. "Wait. You read my book?" She wasn't sure if she was more surprised that he'd read it or that he could, in fact, read.

He didn't answer, simply stared at her with those soulless eyes.

"What is that." She gestured to the book in his hands, and he threw it on the bed.

Ana picked it up and examined it. *The Lox Empire.* She certainly hadn't read this book before. It didn't even look familiar. "Where did you get this?"

Maddoc didn't answer.

She flipped through it slowly. "Is this a story or a report?"

She glanced up at Maddoc but he didn't reply, that harsh and intrusive gaze remaining on her, unrelenting.

With a sigh, Ana threw the book back on the bed. He was already being an annoying ass. Whatever point he was trying to make made no difference to her. All that mattered was that she stuck to the two things she was withholding for the night.

"Take off your dress," Maddoc said slowly, his gritty voice heavy with obvious desire.

So many retorts sprung to Ana's mouth, but she held her tongue, and annoyingly had to ignore the swirl of arousal in her stomach.

Maddoc tilted his head toward the window. It was almost dusk. "If you don't want your dress torn, I suggest you start taking it off now."

His eyes were making her nervous again, so she shifted her gaze to the window. Today seemed less bright than yesterday.

A low harsh growl erupted in the room, drawing her attention back to Maddoc. His whole body was tense as he looked at her, the fierceness of his gaze blended with either annoyance or anger. Ana almost whimpered at the sound, but she bit her tongue and watched him, trying to divorce herself with the apprehension and overwhelming need that rose with his growl. Her slick was already abundant between her legs, but she firmly ignored it. Her body wasn't within her control around him, and she refused to allow her emotions to get involved *again*.

She kept her eyes on the sky as it darkened further, ignoring the bitterness seeping into the air from Maddoc's anger.

As soon as the day shifted to dusk, Maddoc shot forward, grabbed her around the waist and slammed her back against the wall; his face was close to hers.

"Are you trying to provoke me, Analisa?" he growled as he tore at her dress. "I told you to take this fucking thing off."

Ana was forced to cling to him. "Now that it is dusk, I will do whatever you ask of me until dawn."

Maddoc glared down at her. "You think you can decide when you listen to me and when you don't?"

Ana shook her head. "You have me for three *nights*," she said evenly. "And I did not choose that."

Maddoc pulled her from the wall and threw her onto the bed, scowling. "That doesn't answer my question!"

Ana curled herself in protectively as he advanced toward her, but he flipped her onto her stomach and grabbed the back of the neckline of her dress. A harsh ripping and cool air signified he tore away the back of the dress again, but Ana was prepared for it this time. At the sound, her nipples hardened until they were painful, and her slick gushed from between her legs. It annoyed her to admit that she liked the aggression.

Maddoc wasted no time in pulling her hips up so she was positioned on her knees, then he climbed onto the bed behind her. Grabbing her neck and her hip, his thick tip bumped into her slit, eager to enter, and Ana arched her back and spread her knees wider to welcome him in, desire bounding through every inch of her body.

When he slammed in, hard and rough, she squealed in both delight and surprise. She'd almost forgotten how big he was, how that tang of pain, tempered by a glut of potent pleasure shot up her when she was being split apart. He drove right into the hilt, making her twitch slightly. The burn between her legs, the depth at which he reached, how full she was when he was inside her, all contributed to the raw sensations that pushed every thought from her mind. She tilted her hips, rotating them and clenching down on him, moaning at the pleasure the action bought. The Alpha didn't make her wait long. He drove into her again and again, slamming his hips hard against her ass as he took her, as if he had been waiting to fuck her for years and not only a day. His hand brushed around to her stomach, reaching up to fondle her nipples, and slid down to stroke her clit, while the hand by her neck wound into her hair.

Maddoc fucked her rough, then rougher until she was screaming at the brutality of his thrusts, pleasure and pain battling for dominance viciously within her. When her orgasm approached, it was in an overwhelming rush of sensation that made her body seize and collapse.

When her senses came back to her, the Alpha was still pounding on top of her as she lay flat on her stomach on the bed, his body slapping hers as he sought his own release. Ana widened her legs and pushed her ass back up to meet him, prolonging the sweet sensation of her lingering orgasm.

The Alpha groaned as he thrust sharply, ramming the enlarged base of his cock into her and locking himself to her.

Panting hard, and stretching out on the bed, Ana enjoyed the sensation of being knotted. Last night, she hadn't paid much attention to it, only noticing the discomfort of being permanently stretched wide by an overly large piece of flesh, but there was some comfort to it beyond the physical. It felt instinctively *right* for him to be locked to her in such a way, and previously she'd enjoyed the closeness of his body and the way he touched her while they were knotted. In this instance, he propped himself up on his elbows, his body hovering over hers as they lay catching their breaths.

Maddoc played with her hair, and then lowered his mouth to suck on her ear. She sighed, sinking into this feeling of comfort, but keenly aware she was going to refrain herself unlike last night. So she simply tried to enjoy it.

Maddoc kissed behind her ear and down her neck, and then across her shoulders. After a long moment, he raked fingers along her scalp, causing her to moan with pleasure from his touch.

"Where is my purr, Analisa?" he murmured, after a long moment, nuzzling his nose behind her ear.

Ana's eyes snapped open. He'd been *expecting* her to purr? For a moment, she didn't know how to answer. Although, he had repeatedly encouraged it the night before, she didn't realize he would be expecting it from her each time. She turned her head to the other side as she stretched underneath him.

"Analisa." There was a warning in his tone.

Ana kept her body relaxed, forcing herself not to purr.

The weight of the Alpha came down on her, pressing her into the bed with his warm, thick, body and smothering her with his beautifully potent scent. It was one part she couldn't deny about Maddoc, his scent was spectacular. Whether it was his sweat, his cock, his seed, or just his pheromones seeping into the air around him, she enjoyed experiencing it—almost too much. The warmth of him settled her into the semi-state of sleep, but she was mindful of keeping her promise to herself.

The Alpha grabbed the back of her hair, twisting it hard in his hand until prickles of pain scattered along her scalp. "Purr for me." It was a demand, but not one Ana was willing to abide. He couldn't order that of her.

"It's not something I can control," she said.

"You think I believe that?" His breath was harsh against her ear. "You think I cannot make you the way I did last night?"

"I didn't realize that was part of what you wanted from me," Ana said evenly. "Last night was my first time. You cannot expect the same reaction and response from me."

"I can," Maddoc sharply. "And I will have it."

"Why?" Ana tried to keep herself and her tone calm and collected. "It is not yours to experience."

The hand at her hair gripped tight and turned her head around to face him, his eyes burning into hers as a fury rose. "It can *only* be mine!"

Ana chose not to say anything at all. This man had to be the most entitled bastard she'd ever known. He wanted to be able to control her no matter what time of day, and thought he was owed her purr. It was not going to fucking happen. She watched his expression as he became more incensed; amusement flickered through her. If he desperately wanted her to purr, withholding it from him could be the one thing to give her control, just like Mother said.

Unfortunately, Maddoc read the challenge in her eyes. As soon as his knot shrunk, releasing him from the tight grip of her hold. He was fucking her again, this time on her back, with her legs over his shoulders as he bent her in half and slammed her into the bed. Then when she didn't purr again, threw her to the edge of the bed and fucked her, gripping and spreading her ass cheeks as she braced herself on the floor. He fucked her repeatedly, demanding her purr each time, until soon, that no longer mattered.

Their sex was magnificently ravenous. Maddoc bent and twisted and pinned and bound her in any way he pleased, fucking her with a hard desperation as though he hadn't just fucked her the night before. If he was still angry about her lack of purring or not doing what she was told, it wasn't clear as the hours passed. He reveled in battering her little body with his enormous one, and seemed to be intent on dominating and marking her—more so than last night. He rubbed his seed into her skin, her hair, her mouth, and all over her face and neck. He bit into her ass cheeks, her thighs, her stomach, her arms, and her back, each time hard enough to break the skin but not to make her bleed. At first when he did it, she was so annoyed that she slapped him, but then remembered she wasn't supposed to have those angry emotions. So she ignored the pain from the bite and focused on his other attentions on her.

The wet, sticky sloshing from their joining, her harsh breaths and whimpers, and his rough growls were the sinful symphony of his brutal possession of her. And Ana loved every moment of it. Even when he slapped her across the back of her thighs or yanked her by her hair. Each sting of pain deepened every beam of pleasure, and he was so rough and animalistic, it drew out the more instinctive elements of her behavior. At first she didn't realize what a danger that was. She cooed and hummed with her lips against his skin, she licked his nipples and combed her fingers through his thick hair. After one particularly delirious orgasm, she told him he was the most handsome man in the kingdom. He simply grunted and twisted her hip to make her soaking channel squeeze him just right.

It was when he held her under her ass, working her on his cock while standing in the middle of the room, that things changed. She was gripping his shoulders to keep herself steady, her calves draped over his forearms as he pounded into her, when she slid her arms around his neck and leaned forward to press her body to his.

It was such a smooth and natural movement, that when her lips pressed against his, she didn't think anything of it. Until he kissed her back.

Warm and intimate, his kisses were enticingly strong and sensual. A zing of rapture and longing tore through Ana's body, and suddenly this wasn't just about a night of mindless lust.

She tried to pull back quickly, but the Alpha had already wrapped his thick arms around her and pressed her close as he explored her mouth—she couldn't escape.

And then she wasn't sure she wanted to. Having him inside her and kissing her at the same time was so… sexy. It aroused her so much that within moments, her slick was splattering on the floor as he jerked his hips into hers. And when she climaxed, in his arms, on his cock, and with his tongue in her mouth, it was like an invasion of the most euphoric madness, galvanizing her body, mind, and heart.

And that was a problem.

SEVEN

*A*na was furious with herself.

After Maddoc knotted her and carried her to the bed, he lay on top of her, wrapping her legs around his waist and tightening his arms around her torso. She was still trying to process what had just happened, but she knew it wasn't good. Something had changed about their connection in the moment she kissed him, at least for her. She wasn't sure about him. She wasn't sure he felt anything at all, apart from the need to fuck her as brutally as he possibly could. But it was a problem. She wasn't sure how much yet; she'd been too exhausted and too elated from the orgasm that was still trembling through her to make sense of it. So she didn't try.

But now awake, still underneath him and remembering what happened, she was annoyed she kissed him, which made it seem like what was happening between them was more than it was. He held onto her and kissed her back thoroughly and completely, as though he had every right to kiss a princess in such an intimate way. Of course, she couldn't exactly blame him. She was the one who instigated it. *Fucking instincts!*

She sighed, trying to find a more comfortable position under his weight. Even though his knot had shrunk, and his cock had slipped out of her, he still held her tight, his breath calm and heavy, but she knew he was awake too.

"You are forgiven," he rumbled heavily, his eyes closed.

Ana already knew she was going to be annoyed, but she still asked. "For what?"

"Not purring."

Ana's mouth tightened. "It wasn't for you."

"Your purrs can only be for me," he responded, a growl in his tone. "You decided it when you first did it."

"I'm talking about the kiss."

At that Maddoc opened his eyes and peered down at her. A growing storm was in them, wild and unbending, but Ana was too annoyed with herself and his attitude to care. "Then who the fuck was it for?"

"Not you," she replied forcefully, glaring at him.

"Anything and everything you do in here is for me," he barked. "There is no one else fucking here." He lowered his voice to a growl. "I know what is happening here is offending your sensibilities as a princess, but you are an Omega first and foremost. And you are behaving in a way that is natural for your dynamic."

Ana stared up at him, an inkling of dread forming. "And what is happening here?"

Maddoc's gaze held that same intensity as always. He cuddled her tighter to him, and when he spoke it was almost soft. "Can you not tell, Analisa?"

Panic smattered across Ana's chest and her throat started to tighten.

"You are at the highest height of society, and you are opening your legs to the lowest of the low," Maddoc said, answering his own question, his tone suddenly bitter.

When Ana glanced back up at him, his gaze had hardened.

"You are bound to want to reject that you offered those things to me, but it is normal for an Omega."

"And how would you know?"

"How can you *not* know?" he shot back. "It is your dynamic. Omegas submit. Just because you are a princess it does not mean you bow to no one."

"I do not bow to you," she said sharply.

Maddoc released a gruff chuckle. "It was the first thing you did when I walked in yesterday. You didn't just bow, you knelt."

"Because you told me to!"

Maddoc's beard twitched. "Exactly."

Ana seethed for a few moments. She wanted to slap him, but she didn't have the energy. "I don't see how you would know what is natural for an Alpha and Omega," she argued. "There is little literature on it."

"Whatever I want to do as an Alpha," he began, "and whatever you want to do as an Omega, is what is natural. I thought that would be obvious."

"That is a simplistic way of looking at it."

Maddoc shot her a look. "Do you have another?" A mocking tone entered his voice. "Tell me, Analisa, how does the most ignorant Omega in the kingdom determine what is natural between an Omega and an Alpha?"

"I'm not the most ignorant Omega in the kingdom," she snapped.

"You are," Maddoc said bluntly. "Tell me. How do you plan on ruling a kingdom when you've never sat on the council?"

"Just because I turn twenty-two and will marry within the month doesn't mean I will instantly become queen," she replied, somewhat harsher than she intended. "There is time for me to learn. Father is in his prime, I will not succeed him for years, possibly decades. It is you who is ignorant if you think all princes and princesses succeed their parents at twenty-two."

Maddoc said nothing following her retort, but he watched her carefully for a long moment.

Ana held herself tense, waiting for his mocking reply, but when he didn't respond she couldn't keep it up. Relaxing in his arms, she asked, "I suppose you are wholly educated and informed about Alphas and Omegas? Even though there are no significant documents, books, or texts about them."

"I gave you one earlier."

Ana frowned. "Where did you find it."

"That isn't important. The important part is what are within the pages."

"You stole it probably," Ana muttered.

Maddoc didn't answer, but he leaned into her neck and scented her, causing a shiver to run down her spine. Her mind returned to their kiss, desire rising for another one, and suddenly she had something to ask. "Do you have a wife?"

"No."

"*Did* you have a wife?"

Maddoc's glanced down at her with a strange look. "No."

"So you just have whores that you have sex with?"

Maddoc propped himself up on his elbow as he watched her. For the first time, there was a smile in his dark eyes. "You are concerned about whom I fuck."

"No," Ana shot back at him. "I'm just trying to determine how many diseases I've probably caught from you."

His beard twitched. "If I fuck animals, you have already caught a multitude of fatal illnesses. There's no point in trying to figure that out now."

Ana scowled as Maddoc lay back down with a chuckle, pulling her to his hard chest. "What do you really want to know, Analisa?"

She thought for a moment. "Did you send those men to attack Father?"

"No."

She glanced up at him. "How did you know about the attack, then?"

"We were watching them. They weren't familiar to Allandis and I wanted to know what they were doing here."

Ana swallowed slowly. For Maddoc to be watching them, he would have to have men all over Allandis. That was almost unbelievable considering how big the kingdom was. "Why did you save Father?"

"I explained that in court."

She pursed her lips thinking back to the court hearing. "He could have killed you as soon as you arrived here, before knowing anything about the debt. Why did you risk it?"

"If Orick killed me as soon as I arrived, he wouldn't be able to revel in the glory he would get from declaring me a criminal in front of his precious court. Killing me quietly is not his style—I knew it wouldn't happen."

Ana suddenly realized that Maddoc called her father by his name. Never "His Majesty," or even "the king." He hated her father that much? She shook her head slowly at the animosity between the two men. Even if Maddoc hated her father, any man with that much power outside of the royal assembly could do so much good, and yet Maddoc chose not to. "Why are you doing this?" she asked quietly. "Why are you so willing to destroy my life specifically? I know you don't care about the hurt you cause across the kingdom, I know you don't care about the towns you sacked, and I know you don't care about the royals. But why me—specifically?"

"Your life will not be destroyed."

"You know it will," she snapped, annoyed he was still treating her like an idiot. "You don't care because you don't value it, like you don't value anything. You think I'm a fool and an idiot who doesn't—"

Maddoc leaned down and pressed his mouth against hers in a rough, hard kiss. Instantly, the anger that was building turned into a fierce, savage hunger. Maddoc kissed her like he fucked her—deep, volatile, and dominating, yet there were moments that were so sweetly tender, it left Ana breathless. He played with her nipples until she was moaning into his mouth, begging for more. Within moments, Maddoc had her on his cock, riding him while he pulled her head back and sucked her neck, her ear, her breasts, anywhere he could reach, before returning his tongue to her mouth.

Their mating had a different mood to it now. It was still frantic and raw and carnal, but now there was a stormy, irresistible feel to it that hadn't been there before... and Ana was powerless against it.

When Ana woke again, she was pinned under Maddoc's arm and leg. She lay still, quieting her thoughts, and trying to figure out what she was supposed to do now. She clearly failed in her attempt to withhold her emotions, although she succeeded in withholding her purr. But in the end, she had done something far worse—and now everything between them felt different. She didn't like it.

Even though Mother had advised her to withhold things that made her vulnerable, the purpose was to try to control him with it, to try to get information out of him. But she just couldn't see how.

She sighed and slowly crept out of bed. Heading over to the table, she drank her fill of the water, eying the plates of food. He'd left the food untouched this time, too concerned with fucking her when he first arrived, but that didn't mean he still didn't bring whatever he used last time. Ana padded over to the pile of his clothes, and keeping an eye on him, searched for his furs. His clothes were enormous and in the semi-darkness of the room, it was impossible for her to figure out what item she grasped. Only halfway through searching when he stirred, she quickly abandoned the task.

Her heart pounded as he turned over and reached for her.

"Come here." His gruff voice lurched into the room.

Ana headed toward the bed, but as she neared her foot kicked something on the floor. The book he had given to her was by the underside of the bed. Picking it up first, she then slid back into the bed, and the Alpha engulfed her in his thick arms and kept her pressed against his chest. As she lay there, she marveled at the way he slept—holding her in his arms and completely unafraid. Did he sleep with all his woman the same way? Surely, there were some, more capable than her, who would take advantage of a slumbering outlaw—steal his money, try to kill him for the constant bounties placed on him. She traced his nose with her finger. It had only been two nights, and yet things felt so... she pushed the thoughts aside.

Using the moon's light streaming through the window, she thumbed through the book she picked up.

It was difficult to know whether it was a story or a recounting of factual events. As she continued flicking through it, she realized it was about an Alpha and Omega. She carefully sat up and examined the book, turning it over in her hands to see how and where it was made. It was a simply bound book with nothing on either cover nor the spine, and no insignia of the bookmaker, which was strange. She started from the beginning and began to read.

Ana was almost halfway through when Maddoc stirred again. His hand brushed over her hips, swept down the back of her thigh and hooked under her knee to lift her leg and place it on his shoulder. When his lips caressed the inside of her thigh, her breath hitched.

He was already looking at her, that beautiful darkness in his eyes, and she slowly reached out a hand to brush the pads of her fingers over his dark bushy brows. He had such a distinctive look, and one that affected her in a way she never thought possible. Her finger trailed down his face to his beard, and she caressed his cheek slowly. He was definitely a handsome man, but in a different way from the other Alphas she knew. He wasn't refined like those of the royal houses and was more rugged than Alphas who were soldiers or farmers. But that didn't make him any less appealing, in fact, he was very attractive.

They stared at each other in comfortable silence for a long while, Ana taking her time to stroke the hair on his chin, brushing her thumb over his mustache while he stared at her with that dark desire.

"I'm reading the book you gave me. You didn't tell me it was an Alpha and Omega couple story," she said finally, drawing her hand away.

Maddoc lowered his head again and kissed the inside of her thigh, sweeping his tongue along her skin as he headed inward, but he said nothing.

"It's filled with magical portals and orbs and shields," she said, unable to hide the smirk in her tone. "I didn't realize you believed in magic. I thought *I* was the one who believed in children's folktales."

Maddoc lifted his eyes to hers. "It is rare, but it does exist."

Ana had to stop her mouth from dropping open. "You believe in magic?" She would have laughed if his expression wasn't so serious. "Magic does not exist!"

Maddoc kept his eyes on her and resumed his journey up her thigh.

Ana stared at him. "You really believe in magic?"

"There are pockets within the kingdom where unusual people and unusual things exist. Sometimes there is no explanation for them except to believe the unbelievable."

Ana scoffed and shook her head, but didn't know what to say. Who would believe that the notorious outlaw Maddoc believed in magic? But at least now she had a way in to a topic her parents might want to know about. "You've traveled all over Allandis?"

Maddoc nodded.

"It's never been fully charted."

"No," Maddoc said pointedly. "Because some places cannot be reached without believing the unbelievable."

Ana had to smile and Maddoc immediately lifted his head to watch her.

"What was your favorite place?"

"Right here."

Ana did laugh at that. "Here? In the palace? Among people who want you imprisoned?" She shot him a look. "I find that hard to believe."

Maddoc said nothing, but his eyes had a softness to them as he watched her. And that made her nervous.

"Is the Oakenshire forest as wild as they say it is?"

"Yes."

"Do all your men also believe in magic, fairies, and folktales?"

Maddoc growled in annoyance. He rose from the bed and headed toward his pile of clothes. Searching through them, he lifted his pants and dug his hand into the pocket to collect something, then approached the table of food and indicated for her to follow.

Ana scrambled off the bed and did as instructed, apprehension growing in her stomach. Father surely would have poisoned the food by now, and even though she had been completely fine with the idea of poisoning him earlier that day, the idea of it now was... unsettling.

Maddoc held out his hand again, and in the center of his palm sat a large blue pebble. It didn't look like it anything she recognized and was an unusual color, almost as though it were a gem. "This was created for me by a woman whose life I saved," Maddoc said. "It detects harmful substances."

"How is it able to do that?"

"When I hold it near poisonous or toxic substances, no matter how small a dose, it burns bright blue."

Ana laughed nervously. "Is that what you were doing yesterday?"

Maddoc nodded. "Yes, I was checking if the food was poisoned. It seemed too good to be true for the king to feed me, although I've made it quite difficult for him to kill me outright, at least for now." He turned to face the table holding out the pebble in his palm.

Ana watched his face to see how much he truly believed what he was saying. There's no way this could work.

To her utter surprise, the pebble began to shine blue almost immediately. She gasped and Maddoc stiffened. He held his hand over the table, watching the stone, and it glowed when hovered over every dish, even over the mead. But when he moved his hand over the water, it faded back to its normal blue color.

"It seems the king was trying to trick me into a false sense of security," Maddoc said, his voice low. "The man has no honor."

Ana frowned. "Because he tried to poison an outlaw?"

"Because he's supposed to be honoring the Royal Promise," Maddoc barked. "He shouldn't be trying to kill me by sneaking poison into my food while he is paying off a debt. He will have to suffer for this." Maddoc growled, turning from the table agitated. "I wonder sometimes if I should bother waiting for his demise. I should just kill him."

Ana's stomach plummeted. Fear twisted back into her stomach, along with a heavy dose of annoyance. "You won't succeed."

Maddoc turned to her, his eyes blazing. "Anything I want to do, I do it."

"Then why didn't you?" she said sharply. "You keep insinuating you can kill him any time you want; you claim you had the opportunity to do so when he was injured. Why didn't you then and why don't you now? I'm starting to think you can't do anything to him, only find ways of punishing other people to make him suffer." She huffed out a breath as her heart pounded in her chest. "Instead of using other people, and causing them pain, why don't you just do it?"

"Have you ever heard me say I want to kill the king?" Maddoc thundered.

"It's obvious you do. It's what you tell the villagers, and it's the point every time you strike a blow at the crown," Ana said hotly.

"This is what makes you ignorant," Maddoc said, stepping toward her. "You believe everything you're told, you do everything they say, you don't learn things for yourself or try to make sense of the illogical facts they present to you. Lies upon lies upon fabrications dominate this kingdom. You even watch them," he accused. "You watch them playing their games of gossip, and yet you believe that everything you are told is the truth." His expression was of such disgust that Ana flushed.

"Are you saying that you never did any of those things?" Ana asked, knowing she wouldn't believe him if he said no.

Maddoc said nothing for a moment. He took another step and she stepped back at the same time, the tension between them so thick it was like being tethered to lightning. "It is how it is presented," he said finally.

Ana blinked. *Wasn't that what Mother said?*

"For example," Maddoc continued, "do you agree you are a whore?"

Ana ground her jaw so hard she was surprised her teeth didn't crack. "*No*, I don't fucking agree."

"And yet, even though you've come here against your will, you open your legs to me and accept me between them without question," Maddoc said. "I present you with my cock and you open your mouth and drink whatever I give you, you moan and scream and touch and caress me, you urge me to fuck you, wriggling those sexy hips and spreading your legs wider to tease me with that sweet slit."

Ana stared at him horrified. "That's not—"

"Those are the *facts*!" Maddoc thundered. "And even if they weren't, it would be easy to imply. Tell me, would you call a woman doing all those things a whore?"

Ana's face burned so hot she could barely breathe. She pressed her palms to her cheeks to cool them down, but she couldn't take her eyes off Maddoc. "It's not the same situation."

"It's exactly the same. It's even predictable." Maddoc grabbed her, pulling her against his body. "I already know that when I touch you here," he said, brushing his hand over her nipple and tweaking it, "your slick will perfume the room. If I put those nipples in my mouth, the potency of your slick triples, and makes me harder than I've ever been before."

"Stop," Ana begged quietly, lowering her eyes, mortified.

He dropped his hand to her mound and tickled along her folds. "I know that if I yank your hair while your hips are tilted just the right way, you will come so beautifully and squeeze my cock so hard, you will dominate my thoughts for hours."

Ana swallowed, trying to come to terms with what he was saying. "I don't care if I'm your whore now. I won't always be."

Maddoc peered down at her but she couldn't look him in the eyes. She had been trying so hard to justify the way he'd made her feel, but he was right, it could be simplified down to one simple truth: she was his whore. It wasn't like she didn't know that would happen when this started. He'd wanted to humiliate her, embarrass her, and ruin her—and that's what he'd done. She couldn't stop him from telling people that… if he survived her father's attempt to kill him.

"Even if my reputation never recovers from this, after tomorrow night, you will go on your way, and I'll marry my fated mate," she said trying to cling on to the hope that Ryden would still want her. "I'll do all those things with him, and I won't be a whore then."

Maddoc's fingers on her slit froze. "He is not your fated mate."

"It was arranged," she explained. "We have been paired."

"I don't give a fuck. It is a lie."

"And how would *you* know?" Ana asked, irritably.

"How can you *not* know," he bellowed.

Ana jerked, surprised at his sudden anger. "I haven't… been with him yet. I'll know as soon as I am—it should be better than being with you."

Maddoc roared, veins pulsing in his neck as he grabbed her and lifted her until her eyes were level with him. "There will never be anything better!"

Ana snarled at him, her anger jumping to match his. This man was so arrogant! "Nothing better than being your whore?" she snapped at him. "I'm sure your ego allows you to believe that, but I assure you, it's not true!"

"If I wanted a whore, I could get a different one for each hour of every night." The darkness in his eyes swirled as his gaze clung to her. "It's not about that." He carried her to bed and threw her down. "Do you think you will ever be as aroused as this?" He pried her legs open to reveal fresh slick smeared all over her inner thighs.

Ana hissed and tried to push his hands away but he held on tight, dragging her to the edge of the bed. He positioned himself at her entrance, his mushroomed tip massaging the aching muscles of her entrance that had been waiting for him from the moment she woke. She bit back a moan, but her muscles clenched around him of their own accord, and he sunk in slowly.

"Do you think any other cock could fill you so deeply? So completely?"

At that moment, Ana couldn't imagine it. He was so deep, she was almost breathless. "It's not my choice," she said, with difficultly. "That is how I've been paired."

Maddoc's eyes flashed as he pulled all the way out, then slammed in again. Ana cried out, trying to catch her breath.

"He will not have you," he ground out bitterly as he pulled back, then slammed in again. "You belong to me. You always have."

Ana twisted her torso, surrendering to the blunt force pleasure he served, but tried to keep her mind on what he was saying. "Only... for three... nights," she managed, as her body shunted on the bed from his thrusts.

Maddoc lifted her from the bed and held her firm on his cock as he turned them around. He sat on the bed and wound his fingers into her hair, pulling her back slightly as he looked down on her, the moonlight making his shining eyes almost enchanted. "It was never only for three nights, Analisa."

EIGHT

Maddoc remained infuriated for the rest of the night. He didn't speak to her again, and she didn't dare say anything else or ask him any more questions.

He kept her permanently lodged on his knot, and as soon as he slipped out of her, he was pummeling her with his cock again. There was a vicious edge to the way he handled her now, as though he was annoyed she mentioned Ryden or defended her father. He bit her on her breast, hard enough to draw blood this time, and wouldn't let her clean it up. He now slept with her underneath him completely, not allowing her to get up without him knowing.

Ana felt trapped, suffocated by his overbearing behavior and his body. When she panicked from the feel of claustrophobia, a soothing rumbling vibration thrummed from his chest and seeped into her body, helping her to relax. As she drifted to sleep she realized he was purring for her.

Each time she woke up after that, his purr strengthened, settling her underneath him and soothing her back to a sleepy state. She wasn't sure what he meant by *it was never only three nights,* but each time she woke, his words revolved in her mind. If he planned for more, then why the pretense? Were his men orchestrating something while he was in here with her? Was he using her as a distraction for the guards, her parents, and the court, while he did something horrible somewhere in the palace? That seemed to be the most logical conclusion, but how could she figure that out without more information?

As dawn approached, he got up and dressed, then picked up Ana and placed her near the center of the room by the window. She wasn't close enough to see out, but the daylight shone directly on her, which brightened her mood.

Maddoc stood in front of her, his eyes roaming her face as she looked up at him. "I will answer all of your questions at dawn tomorrow."

Ana nodded, but she knew that by dawn tomorrow, it would be too late. The king had already planned for something terrible to happen to Maddoc. She wasn't sure how she felt about it now that she'd spent time with him. Was it foolish that she didn't want him to die?

"Don't punish Father for the food, Maddoc. Please."

He held her eyes for a moment. "Do you think if it were reversed, he would spare me?"

Ana's face dropped. No, of course he wouldn't. Father had wanted to kill Maddoc for years. "But you are an outlaw. You might not like it, but you break laws. You can't compare yourself to my father."

"You are not one who can make that comparison, Analisa." His gritty voice was tinged with annoyance. "You have no knowledge of what your father does on a daily basis, the decisions he makes, the people who are effected by it."

"I do. I watch court hearings all the time."

Maddoc shot her a look. "Have you ever turned up to one unannounced?"

Ana frowned. "What difference would that make?"

Maddoc didn't answer, but his gaze never left her, and a twinge in her stomach made her wonder if she really wanted him to.

"You said you wouldn't kill him," she mumbled, her eyes low.

"And I won't."

Ana, grateful for that, dipped her head.

Maddoc used a finger to tilt her chin up. "Remember, no one is to touch you."

Ana almost rolled her eyes. "I'm not sure why you think I'm engaging in all of these sexual activities. I can barely survive nights with you."

Maddoc's beard twitched. "Sex is a commodity in Allandis high society, Ana."

Ana nodded, she'd always known that. "But why would I do anything with them?"

"Being a virgin doesn't mean that you don't trade other favors."

Ana thought back to the way he had ordered her to her knees the previous night. He'd been checking if she'd had any prior experience before.

As if he read her mind, Maddoc slowly lowered to his knees, Ana's eyes widened, unsure what he was doing, but when he leaned forward and pressed his nose to her mound, she let out a breathy moan. "Maddoc," she whispered.

His tongue brushed her folds, stroking them gently before pressing his mouth farther in and sucking, flicking and grazing everything he could reach.

Ana moaned, pleasure racking her body as his mouth closed over her clit. She ground her hips in her his face, tilted them and spread her legs to give him more access. He set a steady rhythm, brushing and swirling his tongue until she was climbing that breath-stealing peak. His hands squeezed her ass, pulling her closer to him; her hands were in his hair, grabbing handfuls as the pleasure built.

Just as she was about to tip over the edge, Maddoc pulled away and rose to his feet, those intense eyes back on her.

Ana panted, frowning. "Why did you stop?"

Maddoc tilted his head toward the window, and when Ana turned to it, she was almost blinded by the sun. It had just broken over the horizon and was streaming through the window. Ana almost cursed. *The damn sun!*

Maddoc leaned in so close, she could smell herself on his glistening lips.

"I will finish at dusk tonight," he murmured. "And I will know if you have touched yourself, so don't."

Ana rolled her eyes in amusement. So she couldn't even touch herself. She should have guessed. Strangely, the idea of seeing him at dusk was exciting. Having him kneel before her like that, giving her pleasure with his mouth while she stood, had to be one of the sexiest and erotic things she had experienced with him.

She nodded, and Maddoc glanced down at her lips. She wondered if he wanted to kiss her as badly as she wanted him to, but they couldn't touch each other now.

After a long moment, he picked up her dress and walked out.

Milly came to collect her again, this time armed with appropriate gowns, shawls, and hats. She was pleased to see that Ana wasn't as distressed as the first night, so she left her alone to bathe while summoning her parents.

Ana took her time bathing, glad to wash off the sweat, dried semen, and crusted blood. She didn't feel as achy as last night, but her body still pained her a little. Her mind was busy mulling over Maddoc's behavior. The most concerning thing for her was his implying he'd planned to extend their nights together. Father certainly wouldn't allow it, but Maddoc was not stupid—and would have known that. She wondered if he planned to kidnap her, but that didn't make sense either. And why would Maddoc, who traveled all over the kingdom, steal a princess who would be recognizable anywhere she went? It wouldn't be smart to have her live as an outlaw like him, so what did he mean? She sighed and shook her head.

The most immediate and pressing issue was Father killing him at dawn tomorrow. At the beginning, she didn't think twice about his impending death, but now... she wasn't sure she could be part of that—not without at least warning him. Maddoc was forceful, brutish, crude, and rude when he wanted to be, but there were moments, like this morning, when he was almost perfect, and that in itself was amazing. She never expected to find even one part of him desirable or worth of a second thought, but he was more complex than Ana realized.

She knew, though, that she couldn't expect Mother and Father not to take the opportunity to kill him if they had the chance. She may have found some qualities in him she liked, but she wasn't so blinded that she didn't realize they were largely due to her instincts as an Omega. She didn't know the man apart from what she'd experienced in the room, and he had done some terrible things over the years. In that sense, warning him seemed foolish.

Mother and Father arrived after her bath and sat where they had yesterday morning—the queen on the chair facing the bed, the king standing slightly behind her, and Ana sat on the bed.

"You seem to be doing much better this morning than yesterday morning," the queen remarked, her eyes roaming over her daughter carefully.

Ana nodded. "I think I'm getting used to it."

"You shouldn't have to get used to that," the king growled.

"Did you remember all things we talked about," the queen asked.

Ana inhaled a breath and nodded. "I wasn't that successful," she admitted.

The queen smiled. "That's all right. Sometimes it takes time to get ahold of our own instincts and emotions. I'm sure you'll do much better tonight. Tell us what happened."

Ana shrugged. "I'm not sure how much there is to tell," she admitted. "Much of it was similar to last night, except he was more focused on me than the table."

"It looks as though he didn't eat at all?"

Ana shook her head. "He has a method of determining whether his food is safe or not."

The king lifted his brow while the queen inclined her head. "How?"

"Magic."

Both the king and the queen stared at her, clearly as shocked as she had been. "Magic?" the queen finally said. "Maddoc uses magic?"

"I don't know how extensively he uses it, but he does believe in it, and he was able to use it last night to figure out that everything on the table was poisoned, except for the water."

The king's frown deepened, while the queen's shoulders dropped. "So he ate nothing at all?" the queen asked.

"No."

Her father began to pace across the room, in deep thought. "If he uses magic, it would explain a lot. He could have used it in a variety of ways over the years to escape us or pretend to be in multiple places at once. He's been careful never to make it seem like he's using it so we wouldn't suspect."

"Most people wouldn't suspect that at all," the queen remarked. "Or that magic even still existed."

"Does it?" Ana asked, surprised.

"Supposedly, according to some scholars," her mother answered.

The king turned to Ana. "Does he use magic himself? Or does he have people use it on his behalf?"

"I don't know," Ana said. "It didn't seem like he could do himself, but I don't know."

The king nodded slowly, deep in his thoughts.

"I will say, he wasn't happy about the fact the food was poisoned," Ana added. "He felt that it dishonored the promise."

Father brushed away her words with a swipe of his hand. "The man is a hypocrite. He likes to criticize others about things he cannot and will not do himself. I'm sure many of the towns and villages he robbed would have preferred him to be honorable and not harm their women and children after robbing them."

Ana nodded glumly. After a pause, she asked. "How many villages and towns were there in total?"

The king blinked at her enterprising question. "What?"

"How many villages and cities have been affected by him robbing them?"

"Why do you want to know that?"

Ana shrugged. "I thought maybe it might be a good idea to visit them to make sure they are thriving or at least back on their feet by now. I don't recall those places ever being on my route when I go out and visit the people."

"Because there is no need to do any of that, Ana," the queen said. "Much has already been done for most of them, and the newer ones are in very bad condition—not suitable for a princess to visit."

Ana shook her head, annoyed. "How am I supposed to lead if I never visit the places where people are suffering?" She looked at both of her parents, another thought forming in her mouth that she knew would change things between them if she let it out.

"You can accompany us the next time we go," her mother said, nodding in agreement. "Is there anything else you can think of about last night?"

Ana thought back. She wasn't willing to tell anybody about the Alpha and Omega book he'd given her. There was something about it that struck her as strange, and she wanted to follow her intuition about it before she told her parents.

"Did he take your dress again?" the queen asked.

Ana nodded. She hadn't even bothered to ask him why he kept taking them, he was obviously selling them to the highest bidder, no doubt claiming they were hers. People were more likely to believe him now that he was coming in and out of the palace. "He did say something strange last night," she said finally. "He suggested it would be more than three nights."

"I'm sure he fucking did," the king growled. "Bastard! That is all he is getting."

"We have arranged for his death at dawn tomorrow," the queen said stiffly, as if that solved everything.

Ana lowered her gaze, twisting her fingers together in her lap. "Is there any way we can simply imprison him?"

Her mother smiled at her sadly. "No, Ana. I know he seems more real to you now than before all of this happened, but he is still a criminal, and he must pay for his crimes. If we were to imprison him, it is likely his men will attempt to rescue him."

"Multiple times," the king added. "Causing danger for all of us."

"He has already committed enough crimes to be executed ten times over. This is a kindness to his future victims."

Ana nodded glumly. It would be difficult to try to save a man with crimes like that, but it was strange to her how he always questioned the validity of the things she accused him of—as if she'd gotten it wrong. She'd hoped that meant he didn't do some of things they accused him of, and there wouldn't be enough time to find the truth if he died tomorrow.

The only decision that remained was if she was going to warn him.

After Mother and Father left, Ana visited the library, taking Maddoc's Alpha and Omega book with her.

Once her guards had cleared the library, she began an intensive search for any books that were similarly nondescript. As well as lacking a bookmaker insignia, *The Lox Empire* didn't have any cover cloth or author name or even a published date, so she had no idea how or when the book came into existence. But if there were more stories about Alpha and Omega couples, potentially in the library, those might have more details.

There were, of course, many stories written about Alphas and Omega's separately, as well as many factual retellings and reports. But there were none that Ana had seen about a couple. Until now.

Ana paused when she came across a book that didn't match its cover cloth. The cover read; *Two Thousand Tales from the Oakenshire*, but the book itself was too thin to fit the title. She flicked through it, and the story inside seemed to be a factual retelling of an Alpha and Omega couple who once ruled Allandis.

Stunned, Ana carried the book to her favorite chair and began reading. It was a thrilling tale about a couple who ruled Allandis like her parents did. Of course, she'd heard about them; she was descended from them, but to read their stories as though she was right there with them was extremely exciting. And what adventures they had! Their love and passion shone through the pages, and it even included diary entries of the couples' thoughts about each other, including their intimate times.

Ana glanced at her guards to make sure they wouldn't notice her reddening, but she was too engrossed in the story to stop. Maddoc had one thing right: stories with sex were much more intriguing.

After closing the book, she headed to one of the walls that depicted her family tree, searched for their names, and grinned when she found them. They had been a handsome couple. As she surveyed the other ruling couples, most of whom had been Alpha/Omega couples, Ana realized that it was probable there were other retellings of the other ruling couples of Allandis, who would most likely come from her line.

She began to search the library with renewed efforts, trying to find the books that had unusual covers or where the covers and titles didn't match the contents, but it was difficult considering the library was so big. Ana first headed to the boring sections of the library where she never really browsed; they were sections Milly never recommended for her studies, and within an hour, she'd found five more and each story was a retelling, and just as interesting and passionate as the first.

A heavy disappointment weighed down on Ana's chest. Why were these stories hidden? What was the purpose of lying about what was in a book, creating a different cover to what was in the contents? Why were these stories of her family history never included her lessons? Why did her mother lie and say there wasn't much text about Alphas and Omegas being together? So many questions flooded her mind, and it all seemed to support what Maddoc had told her. But how had he known the stories were here?

The sixth book she found made her almost feel ill. It was very similar to the one that Maddoc gave her; it wasn't clear if it was a story or a factual retelling; however, the Omega's name in the book was Atara, like her mother.

Apprehensive about what she was going to find, Ana settled into her chair and read it.

In the book, the Omega princess came from a different kingdom. She was destined to marry an Alpha from her kingdom, but there was no arranged marriage or pairing, like in Allandis. Alphas had to fight to impress the Omega; demonstrating skill, strength, and wisdom to prove that he was the most appropriate male for her. The Omega, Atara, had been the youngest princess of the ruling family, and a series of battles had been arranged for an entire week to determine who she was going to marry. Even though those battles took place, Atara found herself in love with the son of an Alpha from a different kingdom who'd visited that week in hopes of making an alliance with her father.

Ana's heart began to pound but she kept reading. Atara and the visiting Alpha's second son fell in love within moments of meeting, but there were only two days left of the tournaments. The king wouldn't break tradition for her to marry whom she wanted, even though a marriage across kingdoms was the best way to secure an alliance. So, the night before the final tournament, Atara vanished, never to be seen again. It was speculated she traveled to Allandis where she joined one of the royal houses and bribed the pairing scholars to "arrange" for her to marry the second son of the ruling king.

Ana closed the book, her heart in her throat. This couldn't be about her mother—Mother simply could not have come from an entirely different kingdom. But hadn't someone sent men to kill the king? Was it an assassination attempt from another kingdom that had allowed Maddoc to save the king that day? Who had the men been? And why would they be trying to kill her father?

Suspicion, annoyance, and curiosity cascaded into Ana's mind as she realized how much she truly didn't know and how much she hadn't been told. The worst part was that she never questioned it, just simply took whatever she'd been told at face value. She could almost hear Maddoc's voice in her ear calling her ignorant. She looked at the text in her hand, dread making her mouth bitter. If this was truly her mother, then she had been lied to about a lot of things, but what was the point? What were her parents, or particularly her mother, trying to hide? She looked down at the books in her lap. What was the connection between them? They were all about ruling

Alpha and Omega couples, but their stories were all slightly different. Apart from the one about her mother, they all went through the arranged marriage process to find their fated mate. What was there to hide? Gritting her teeth in annoyance at her inability to piece the puzzle, Ana returned the books back where she found them, taking note of where they were so she could find them again.

She might have been ignorant and blind to a lot of things going on, but her mother wasn't. And she would have to ask her.

"Ana." The queen smiled widely and patted the seat next to her. She was preparing to visit a nearby village for a minor event and sat in front of a mirror in her bed chamber while handmaids added little gold hearts to the golden headpiece that rested on her blonde hair. "I was going to come and see you again today. I heard that you were back in the library."

Ana didn't return her smile. "I was," she said. "I was reading an interesting story about an Alpha and Omega couple."

The smile remained on her mother's face, but the look in her eyes changed. She raised a hand, and her handmaids ceased their task and left swiftly. "Interesting. Where did you find that?" she asked casually.

"In the library. There are many in there it seems."

The queen's smile faded. "Then how did you find them?"

"Does it matter?" Ana asked. "I just want to know why they are hidden, and if they are true?"

"I doubt any of them are true," Mother responded. "They are most likely stories for entertainment."

Ana held her gaze, but she was unable to tell if her mother was lying. She always looked calm and mild-mannered, even when she wasn't. That was something Ana had always admired about her, which was also the reason she was able to fool her.

"There is a story in there about a woman called Atara from another kingdom," she began. "A kingdom that had no system of arranged marriages."

Her mother turned paler than normal. "In the library?"

"Yes," Ana said nodding. "And it details how she met an Alpha from Allandis, and then traveled here and inserted herself into a royal house so that she could marry him."

The queen rose from her seat and paced across the floor, her composure gone.

"Is it you?" Ana asked, evenly.

"No," her mother breathed, distracted by her thoughts, her hand on her forehead as she came to a stop by the bed.

Ana looked at her closely, and it was clear she was disturbed. She was pale and slightly sweaty, and the hand on her forehead shook.

"I need you to find me that book and bring it to me," her mother said after a moment.

"No," Ana said simply. She rose from her seat. "When you stop lying to me, I'll give it to you."

"Ana." The anguish in her mother's voice tore at her resolve, but she was too angry she'd been lied to, even now. "Please understand," her mother said. "There is more going on here—"

"You said that before!" Ana shouted in annoyance. "There is always more going on than me just getting the answers I want. I'm not a child anymore, Mother!"

"All right," her mother said, sighing heavily. She wiped the perspiration from her forehead with the back of her hand, and then sat back down next Ana. "It's not my story," she began. "But it is my great, great grandmother's story. She came from another kingdom after having met her fated mate who was from here. As far as I know, she did not bribe her way into being paired with him; she joined one of the houses, and then submitted herself to the pairing process to see if it would work, and it did. It paired her with the Alpha she had fallen for. It was proof that the arranged marriage process works. I don't know if she bribed her way to be with him, but that's not the way I heard it."

"Which house did she join?"

"Redcrest," her mother said. "We have had a long-standing history of allegiance with Redcrest."

"Why would they accept a random Omega from a far-away kingdom?"

"Why wouldn't they?" her mother shrugged. "She was an Omega princess who could give them access to the crown."

Ana nodded. Everything was always about the crown. "Why did you lie to me about stories about Alphas and Omegas. Is it because of this? Do you think people wouldn't understand about your grandmother being from another kingdom?"

"No, it's not because of this, although this could potentially ruin us as well. My grandmother would have been heavily influenced to specifically seek out

Redcrest to join, probably by her Alpha. It was done secretly without any of the other houses having the option to persuade her to join them, which gave Redcrest a significant advantage. That kind of discrepancy, if discovered, could throw our whole claim to the crown into question. The other houses would not take too kindly to that kind of deception." She paused. "Is this something that Maddoc told you about? Is this his plan?"

Ana shook her head. "No, he didn't tell me about your grandmother's story. He didn't tell me why he was doing this, Mother. He keeps implying that I must find things out for myself. I don't think this story has anything to do with him, but it is making me aware that I have been lied to, and I want to know why."

"I'm sorry about lying, but it was for a good reason." Her mother's brows came together slowly, as her whole face changed to one of sorrow. "And I cannot tell you, Ana."

Ana blinked, staring at her in disbelief. "What? Why not?"

"It's for your own good," Amara explained. "To help you have a happy and long life."

"How can I be happy if I know I'm being deceived?" Ana said sharply.

"You were never supposed to question any of this," her mother said, tears glistening in her eyes. "But even though you are, it is better you know you are being deceived into action than knowing the truth."

A nervousness crept into Ana. How could anything be that bad? She huffed out a breath, shaking her head in disbelief that she'd been refused the truth, keeping her in the dark. "I will never trust anything you say," she said through gritted teeth.

Her mother's eyes lowered. "I know. But I'm doing this because I love you. And I will never stop loving you."

Ana didn't know what to make of that, did that mean her mother would never stop lying to her as well? How often has she lied? "Does Father know? Does he lie to me too?"

Her mother nodded, and the betrayal in her chest settled deep.

An enormous bang cracked into Ana's ears, echoing in her chest, and a jolt through the ground shifted her on her chair. She screamed, and her mother grabbed onto her tight. "Are you all right?" she asked.

Ana nodded, though she trembled with fear and her ears pounded so loudly she could barely hear anything. "What's happening?"

The queen rushed to the window, and her hand flew to her mouth. "Something's happened." When she turned to Ana, the shock and horror on her face made Ana's heart stop. "Something's happened inside the grounds."

"What?"

"I can't tell from here." Her mother rushed out of the room and Ana followed her, heading toward the nearest window that overlooked the most extensive and populated area near the royal grounds. Next to the stables, enormous waves of dark grey smoke puffed into the air, surrounding the houses situated there. People were running from them, and some lay on the floor barely moving.

A sickening feeling rolled in her stomach. This had to be Maddoc punishing Father.

"Get her to safety," the queen ordered the king's guard who surrounded them, and before Ana could protest, her guards were rushing her along the corridors. They took her to a secure place in the palace where only her guards knew, separate from the other royals and with an escape out of the palace if needed. Although Ana was annoyed and frustrated to once again be in the dark, this had always been procedure. Luckily she didn't have to wait long before her guards signaled that she could return to her room.

"What happened?" she asked the handmaid who came to check on her.

"There was some kind of blast at the noble houses at the edge of the grounds, Your Majesty," she explained. She looked as though she had been crying. "Some of them lost their lives and others are severely injured."

Ana couldn't breathe. People had died? This wasn't right. For people to die because of the king's actions was unacceptable. She wracked her brain trying to think of who lived in those houses, and her whole body went cold with fear. "Where's Milly?" she asked the handmaid, almost franticly. "Millicent. Where is she?"

"Her family was one of the ones affected, Your Majesty," the handmaid said, tears in her eyes. "Her husband has died, and her son is injured. She is safe," she quickly added. "But her family house was one of those damaged."

Ana was mortified. Milly had been with her husband and lived in her house since before Ana was born. Thankfully, she was alive, but why should she have lost her husband and home because she happened to be a noble? Why should people lose their lives because of it? None of them deserved this. "I want to see her."

It was a few hours before Milly came to visit Ana's bed chamber. She was nothing like the bristly Milly she'd always known. Tears shone in her blue eyes, and her brown hair was in complete disarray. Smoke covered her clothes, her hands were black with soot, and the dark smudges on her face made her expression so haunting.

Ana couldn't help the tears from falling as they spoke for the next hour. Milly was in a complete daze, and it anguished her to see someone who had always been so authoritative look so lost. But based on some of the things Milly hinted at, it was worse than that Ana thought. Now that Milly had lost her husband and her home, she couldn't officially maintain her noble status. She could be retained as Ana's lady-in-waiting as a live-in servant, but she would drop down in the social structure to tradesperson. That meant there was a limit to how much she could earn. With her son also injured, and Milly being an older woman, there were no guarantees she would find her way back to noble status.

Ana was certain she could do something to help, but she didn't know law or procedure.

"You are lucky," Milly said to her, after they both had been sitting in silence for awhile, digesting what had happened. "At least as queen, you will not be bound to your status through your husband." She looked at Ana. "The Alpha and Omega kings and queens always rule equally as a pair, but nothing else is like that in our society."

That was true. "I wonder why," Ana murmured. "It seems insane that it's not."

Milly shrugged. "Omegas are special, I suppose. And they biologically complement their Alphas. It goes deeper than any other pairing. Maybe the Omega has to be equal or the Alpha can't rule."

Ana nodded. That seemed to make sense. Maybe that was one of the other things that all the stories she'd read had in common.

"I'm so sorry, Milly. I'm so sorry this happened."

Milly patted Ana's back as she hugged her. "I'll be fine. It's not your fault, Ana."

But it was.

As the afternoon wore on, a ball of white fury and guilt burned heavily in Ana's chest. This was a perfect example of the destruction Maddoc caused—this was who he really was. How she could have felt the slightest bit of doubt about the tales about him? Why would he be any different to what she'd heard and read?

As reports came through, the blast had apparently been an accident, but Ana knew differently. Maddoc wanted to be able to come back in tonight. None of his current supporters could justify allowing him back into the palace if he admitted to killing and destroying innocent nobles. Ana knew without a doubt, he was to blame. But he wasn't the only one.

This was her fault too. She didn't explicitly tell her parents about Maddoc's threat, nor did she warn them that he'd boasted about having spies inside the palace. There was no excuse for her withholding that. She'd simply been stupid—she hadn't believed Maddoc, and therefore didn't think it was important to repeat. In the back of her mind, she also didn't want to do or say anything that would inflame the conflict between Father and Maddoc and cause them to start an outright declaration of a violent war or kill each other, but Maddoc was not her Alpha nor her husband. He wasn't even her lover. He had manipulated everyone so he could get her in a room with him, and then used her like a whore to get back at her father. That was what he did; make others suffer because of his hatred of the crown. She shouldn't have believed anything he said, because one thing remained clear; if Ana had warned her father, Milly's family may not be dead and injured, and she may not have been in the situation she was now in.

She brushed away the angry tears in her eyes. Even though she was furious with Maddoc for what he did, she knew there was no point in trying to talk to him about it. He would only get angry, lie, and confuse her… it wasn't worth it. She just had to get through her last night with him and then never see him again. At least he had made her decision easy—she was not going to warn him about Father arranging to take his life. If he managed to survive, it wouldn't matter to her. If he died, it would be at least some sort of justice for Milly. Ana would class her time with him as a sexual learning experience and nothing more. Those nights with him felt like she was a different person in a different time, but that's not who she could be.

She spent the afternoon brushing and rebraiding her hair in preparation for dusk, picked a simpler dress to wear and even did her make-up. It was remarkable how different she felt about the situation now that this tragedy happened. Something cold, empty, and hard had lodged into her chest, and it would not be removed.

As dusk approached, there was a knock at her door, and she firmed her mind to deal with him. But when she opened the door, it wasn't her guards. "Ryden?"

Ryden pushed his way into her room and looked around. "You're alone?" He spoke firmly, a serious air about him, and Ana wtached him carefully.

"Yes, what are you doing here?"

Ryden turned to her. His hair had been styled differently, which made him look older, but he wasn't wearing any of his normal clothes. He wore traveling furs, a cape, and had a cloak thrown over his arm.

"I've been trying to see you for the last two days, Ana," he said firmly. "Have you been refusing to see me?"

Ana shook her head. "No. I was in the library today, and yesterday I didn't want to see anyone. I wasn't in the right state, I'm sorry. I couldn't face it."

Ryden strode toward her, and took her hands in his own. "I wish you had let me at least try to comfort you, Ana. I had something I wanted to tell you that might have helped."

Ana eyed him. Something about him was different, he looked more regal, and certainly more resolute. "What is it?"

"Before I tell you, I want to know how you feel about this outlaw."

"I feel nothing for him," Ana said immediately. Something inside her twisted at the words, but she wasn't going to give him the benefit of the doubt anymore.

"You are sure?" Ryden asked, watching her closely.

"Absolutely. He is a criminal."

"Then come with me."

Ana sighed. "We talked about this—"

"We did, but at that time I didn't have the support of Houses Thorneshaw and Goldfrost."

Ana stilled. "What do you mean? Support for what?"

"Support for us to break the Royal Promise and marry now."

Ana's eyes widened. "I don't understand. How can that happen?"

"I can explain it all on the way," he said, handing her the cloak, "but we must go now."

Ana pulled away from him. "I can't risk anything happening to my father because of this. If I'm not there, Maddoc will blame others and hurt people."

"He can blame me," Ryden said bluntly, his upper muscles flexing. "This is not a secret, Ana. I will send a message to your father about what's happening, and our wedding will be announced and celebrated everywhere. If Maddoc wants you, he will have to go through me and at least two other houses to get you, not to mention your father."

"And if he succeeds?" Ana said, slightly panicked. "You will all be dead, and I'll be stuck with him!"

Ryden gently grabbed her shoulders, and stepped close to her, lowering his voice. "I already told you that I want to marry you, no matter what happened with that thug. That is not going to change at any time. I won't give you to this bastard because he is bent on revenge. We have our entire lives ahead of us. We cannot live them in fear."

Ana took a deep breath. Ryden was right, of course. She'd been clinging to the fact that she only had one more night with Maddoc before her father killed him, but if he managed to escape, he wouldn't leave her alone; he'd basically said so. Maybe she should be more proactive and stop being a victim for once.

"Ana?" When she looked up at Ryden, he peered down at her with a hard jaw. "Do you doubt us?"

Ana smiled at him. With all the successful Alpha and Omegas who had been paired the way they had, it was difficult to maintain any doubts about them belonging together. "No. It's just a surprise. Everything feels like it's moving so fast."

"I know, but we were always going to be together, and I shouldn't have let you go through even the first night. I'm sorry."

"It's not your fault, Ryden." And it wasn't hers either. Ana took a deep breath. "All right, let's go."

Nine

MADDOC

The first thing that alerted him something was wrong was that Analisa's guards were not at the door.

Maddoc clenched his fists, tension sparking up his muscles. It was not a good sign. Either they had left her unprotected or she wasn't in there. Either way he wasn't going to be happy. He'd been impressed with the king's attempts to keep her safe. Although his guards were practically useless, he was at least trying, and Maddoc had to be appreciative of that.

Staying alert, he approached the room tentatively, remaining watchful for anything else out of place in the corridor. There were no other doors along this corridor, and it was out of the way for most courtiers, so it had been perfect for his time with his Omega. Only one more night to go.

When he opened the door and entered, he was annoyed to see it empty. Granted it wasn't dusk yet, but Analisa had always been waiting for him. He closed the door behind him, and examined the space. It was exactly the way it had been the last two nights; a table in the far left with food spread out along it, a crude washroom in the corner, and a large bed in the center. The darkening sky had an orange tint to it today and filled the room with a warm glow that would make Analisa's hair look stunning. Her beautiful scent still lingered in the room, and in his nose from when he licked and nibbled her clit this morning. It had been a mistake to get between her legs like that just before they had to leave each other. He'd been rock hard all day, distracted, and fucking irritable. The way she moaned, the way she stroked his hair... *Fuck*. He couldn't wait to claim her. He was even contemplating forgetting the rules and sinking inside her before dusk arrived, but everything had been too carefully planned to start fucking around with things now. So he would wait, cling to his last remaining willpower until dusk. Then he would take everything.

He walked to the window. Nothing looked amiss, and yet everything felt wrong. Analisa should be in here.

When dusk arrived, she had better be in the room or hell would rain down on the king. The only thing that man seemed to have gotten right was producing a woman like Analisa.

Maddoc should have known that she would be different. Of course she was the most beautiful woman in Allandis, but beauty did not always mean anything. He'd been apprehensive about whether she truly was the way she'd been portrayed. Some virginal, innocent child, who they were clearly intending to keep as a child for as long as possible, so the king could hold onto his reign.

Maddoc had seen her visiting villages and towns, talking to the people, playing with children—always pleasant, never a harsh word for any of the commoners, even when they harassed her. But that behavior made her seem dull, with no personality, no fire. And with all that beautiful red hair… what a fucking waste it would have been.

He made it his mission to see her five times before arranging this plan, and she never once strayed from the personality constructed for her. Luckily, Analisa wasn't like that at all.

And in all truth, she never could've been—she was his, after all.

He gritted his teeth as the sky changed, a vicious fury flaring around his body. She wasn't coming.

Maddoc stormed out of the room, holding back the roar he wanted to blare across the whole palace. He couldn't alert anyone yet, not until he got to the king and found out what he'd done with Ana. Then he would suffer.

It didn't take long to gather his men stationed nearby. Within half an hour, they used the known entry points to enter the palace and gather outside the king's throne room.

Even though he was infuriated, it was clear that something was amiss in the palace. Even if Analisa wasn't coming, it was strange to not be greeted by guards, trying to kill him, capture him, or escort him out. It was unlikely the king would allow him to simply roam the palace when he had no reason to be there, regardless of what the people of Allandis thought about his visits. Maddoc tried to be careful and think things through, but anger was coursing through his veins more than any other time in his life. He had been so close, but she had slipped through his fingers. He would need to start again—another three nights.

Once his men were ready, he burst into the throne room and strode to the center, his eyes on the king while his men flanked him. The king sat next to the queen, who looked teary, and a number of their advisors surrounded him.

"I don't have time for you right now, Maddoc," the king snarled, rising from his seat. "This is all your fucking fault!"

King Orick was sending him away instead of killing him? Something was certainly wrong. "What are you talking about?"

"Ana is gone."

Maddoc tensed. "What?"

"She left!" he bellowed. "She's gone to get married, so she can break the promise." He threw a page of parchment at Maddoc, and one of his men collected it for him to read.

The anger that he was barely holding onto nearly erupted as he read it. His woman seemed to think she could play him for a fool. He had warned her multiple times, and yet she had not only chosen to skip their last night, she'd decided to disappear with this idiot of an Alpha who she was betrothed to. He had made himself very clear, and she hadn't listened.

"I don't care what they think. The Royal Promise cannot be broken," he growled, throwing back the note.

"I know that!" The king's face was dark. "If I thought it could be broken, you wouldn't have touched her at all. But it's whatever *you* did has caused her to make this foolish decision." He pointed at Maddoc, snarling. "It is your fault."

For a moment, doubt flickered in Maddoc's chest. Had he been too rough with her, too hard? He didn't try to hold back with Analisa, he didn't need to. He gave her everything, and she had responded with such a beautiful enthusiasm; it encouraged him on. It was even more evidence that he was her Alpha, and she was his Omega. Of course, it was problematic that they didn't agree on anything, apart from how magnificent his cock in her pussy was, but that didn't matter right now. They would have time to figure that out. But this... this was a problem. He couldn't allow any other man to touch her, let alone marry her. She belonged to Maddoc. And her betrothed, Ryden, should have known better. Clearly he had ulterior motives for persuading Ana to do this. There was no way even half the attraction between them was as powerful as what existed between her and Maddoc, and he told her that! The man hadn't even fucked her in the years since it had been announced they were paired. It was unnatural. Still, maybe this situation would provide him with an advantage.

"I will find her," he bit out to the king. "Do not get in my way."

"You will not!" the king roared.

Maddoc roared back, the air in his lungs on fire as he released his rage. This old man thought he could challenge him?! "The promise is still not paid off yet, Orick! Her nights are still mine until it is. So *I* will find her."

"Do you think I give a fuck about your cock?" The king said, incredulously. "Go and find some redheaded whore and pretend she's Ana if you still crave her, but you *will* leave her be or you will be fucking killed."

Maddoc's fingers itched, prompting him to reach for his blade, but he held off. He didn't want to kill the king, but he could still make this work for him. "I will make you a deal."

The king glared at him but said nothing, indicating that he was willing to at least listen.

"If you find her first, the promise is forgotten, the debt is paid. But if I find her first... she is mine."

The king frowned, horror bleeding into his face. "There is no benefit for me to make that deal."

"No? You do realize that once she returns, without this deal, the three nights start from the beginning?"

The king's nose flared, and the Queen began to sob. Maddoc and the king glared at each other for a long moment, until the king broke the gaze, taking a deep breath and exhaling slowly.

"I will agree on one condition," he said. "If Ana does not want to stay with you for longer than a month, you will let her go."

Maddoc almost told him to fuck off. Analisa would not be permitted to leave him. Ever. But what was the use of telling that to the king. He wanted the reassurance his daughter could have freedom if she was still upset after a month, but that was not the way

164

things worked. Still, if he found her first, how would she know?

"Three months."

The king dipped his head in a slow nod. "Deal."

"Deal," Maddoc repeated.

He turned and made his way out of the palace, surrounded by his men. Clearly his Omega was stubborn and disobedient. It would take more work to get her, but he wouldn't have it any other way—she was worth it. But he was furious she hadn't listened. She didn't take him seriously and that had to change, no matter how hard she had to learn that lesson. Maybe it was the days she'd spent away from him that were the problem. Once he got her back, he wouldn't let her out of his sight. He would have his Omega, and the royal court, and all that came with it, could burn.

End of Book One

Turn the page for a sneak preview of
Book 2

A TAINTED CLAIM

Available now

Sneak Peek

Ana

Ana stood in front of the mirror staring at her reflection. The handmaids from Ryden's mansion had done a good job. Not as good as Milly, of course, but at least nothing clashed with the color of her hair.

Tiny gems sewn into the deep emerald wedding gown shone and sparkled with every move she made. The style bared her shoulders, and the long sleeves elegantly tapered and sloped in a style that was highly fashionable in court. The tight corset accentuated her curves, while the skirt puffed out in multiple layers down to the floor. A beautiful train with a lace edge, at least four feet long, spread out behind her in an oval shape. Her crown had been collected from the palace and nestled onto her head. It'd taken two hours to arrange her red-copper locks into a delicate and elaborate hairstyle, showcasing her crown.

In the mirror she looked like a princess on her wedding day, but the confusion and revelations of the last few days dampened her elation and excitement.

This was all wrong.

"Are you ready, Your Majesty?" one of the handmaids asked.

Ana took a deep breath. "As ready as I'm going to be."

The handmaids helped her exit the door where the flower girls were waiting. As Ana turned into the corridor, they positioned themselves either side of her long train.

Since arriving at the Royal Sanctum, the ceremonial building where all royals married, Ana had practiced the route from her room to the altar twice. Ryden had stationed numerous knights along her route, as well as some knights to walk alongside her, which was a fair precaution, but all it did was add further strangeness to the day.

Usually when Ana had visited the venue, the serenity of the place settled her mind and uplifted her heart with a hopeful and romantic mood. Behind the main building was a beautiful garden, and situated at the end of it was the altar, an open structure where couples exchanged their vows. The walk through the gardens signified the shedding of one's old life and the embracing the rigor and beauty of a royal life together. It was a sacred place to wed, and Ana had been looking forward to her wedding day for years; the day she would finally echo the marital vows of her ancestors and every queen who had come before her. But the venue had lost some of its magic. Maybe it was the knights who surrounded her, maybe it was her lingering concerns about Ryden, or maybe the absence of her parents weighed heavily on her. Either way, the idyllic beauty she'd imagined for her day wasn't there.

However, as Ana reached to the top of the stairs where she would begin her walk to the altar, it was hard not to be in awe of the sight of the grounds before her. The altar's legendary gardens spread out, vast and luscious in its abundance, color and greenery. Tables and chairs set with satin emerald and white lace were decorated with flowers. The tables dotted the main area where the invited guests were waiting. A private woodland bracketed the gardens on one side, and on the other was a public viewing area where the Allandis people had gathered to watch, cheering when they saw Ana. Next to the altar, an orchestra played, the melodious strings soaring through the air and finally tugging on her spirits.

Ryden had already made his walk and stood under the thick archway decorated with flowers. She could just about make out his smile as he looked back at her.

At her entrance, the orchestra's music faded and the white-robed herald at the bottom of the stairs cleared his throat. "His and Her Majesties, royal houses, Lords and Ladies, give way for our royal bride, her Majesty, Princess Analisa of Allandis."

Guests from the royal houses and high society all looked upon her expectantly as the orchestra struck up again. Ana took a breath to steady her nerves. This was the most iconic part of all royal weddings—the bride's walk across the gardens. All she had to do was make her way down the steps, through the guests, and to the altar—the guests had even parted to make an aisle for her.

Ana began to descend down the steps keeping her head high. She took in the beauty of the sights before her and tried to draw upon the excitement of the event and ignore the signs that things weren't perfect—such as the large number of knights positioned around the edges of the gardens or that the most important people in her life were not there. Milly wasn't among the guests smiling in encouragement, Mother wasn't standing at the edge of the altar in her favorite ceremonial dress, and Father was not waiting at the foot of the stairs, waiting to assist her along the aisle.

Ana swallowed hard, pushing back the lump in her throat, and kept her eyes on Ryden, reminding herself that this was her true ascension into adulthood. She reached the bottom of the stairs and forced herself to relax as she began her walk.

A series of loud whips followed by muffled puncture sounds disoriented her. Then, all at once, every escorting knight around her fell to the ground, each with an arrow protruding from their chests. Ana froze—a silent horror building as their bodies twitched and jerked. When the flower girls began screaming, the shrill jolted her out of her stupor. Her head snapped up to Ryden, but he was too far away. Around the gardens, knights stumbled, as if attacked by some invisible force, and many dropped down like her guards had.

The guests realized what was happening and their voices rose in alarm as they began to run for shelter. The orchestra stopped playing abruptly, and the din from the crowd of commoners rose.

Ana couldn't help but scream at the horror of the dead bodies that surrounded her. Limp and crooked, some with open mouths of horror or surprise. The Alphas on the ground were men who were supposed to protect her, and terror gripped her at the idea she was so exposed and vulnerable.

She looked around frantically, trying to determine where the arrows were coming from or who was attacking them, but strange men suddenly appeared in the gardens. Huge, bulky Alphas dressed in layers of brown and grey, gripped swords or daggers. Each wore a black cloak with a hood that whipped around them as they attacked the remaining knights. Ana's heart jumped into her throat. Their black cloaks were almost the same as Maddoc's red one.

He was here.

Grabbing her skirts, she ran toward the altar. All she needed to do was get to Ryden and he would protect her—he'd said he could. She could see him looking at the guests and yelling but couldn't hear what he was saying. Just as his eyes landed on her, and relief softened his face, his whole right side jerked backward and he stumbled before falling to his knees, a thick arrow protruding from his shoulder.

Ana screamed, her fear blooming so quickly it overwhelmed her. *No!* Ryden couldn't be shot. She ran harder to get to him, but the guests scattered across the gardens blocking and obscuring her way as they tried to head to an exit.

A bellowing roar of multiple voices filled the air and the crowd slowed in confusion, giving her a chance to see an army of royal knights charge into the gardens from nearly every angle. She almost cried with relief at the sight of the royal insignia on their chests and the flag that rippled above their heads. Her father was here too! A sudden urge to find her father cut through her fear. No matter what happened between them, he would protect her, but she couldn't leave Ryden.

The quickening swish and clash of metal, deep grunts and yells signaled that the gardens had turned into a battleground and screeches filled her ears as the crowd became wilder in their attempt to get away, but she pushed forward unsure if she was still looking for Ryden or seeking out the protection of her father. She wasn't even sure where she was in the gardens anymore, but when a man stepped in front of her, parting the crowd like a rock in a creek, her whole body jolted, her horror turning into pure terror.

Maddoc stood staring at her with those hard, soulless eyes she'd seen when he first entered their room; only this time, the intense anger in them made her mouth dry. That familiar shiver and tremble burst into existence, and she edged backward, words frozen on her tongue.

He strode toward her, their eyes locked as though nothing else existed—as though no men fought and died around them, as though no arrows whipped by their heads. He wore the same layered clothes as before, complete with his red hood, but armor covered his chest and legs and the end of an enormous bow peeked over one of his shoulders. Within moments, he'd closed the gap between them, and as she turned—too late to escape—he swept her up with one arm, her back flush against his chest.

Maddoc turned and strode toward the woodlands on one side of the gardens, calm and relaxed as though he simply came to collect one of his belongings.

Ana held her breath, multiple raw and conflicting thoughts and emotions battering her insides as her mind tried to make sense of what was happening. Behind Maddoc, a battle was being waged in the gardens, every inch of it was filled with men fighting, and a nauseous wave rose to her throat. All this death and destruction. Wherever Maddoc went, this was what happened.

She wriggled in his grip, trying to fight her way out of his hold, but he pressed her tighter against him.

"You will not escape me again, Analisa." His coarse voice was loud in her ear. "Do not even try."

Just as she was about to respond, Maddoc abruptly stopped, his body jerking as the clang of swords rang out behind her.

Ana wriggled out of his grip as he fought, until she was able to slip from his arm, but he grabbed onto her and yanked her behind him as he continued to fight. The king's guard surrounded Maddoc in a close semicircle, engaging him in sword combat but unable to get close enough to her to pull her away from him. Even with one hand, he managed to hold off the kings most trained guards while he held onto her tight.

Looking around for a way to escape, Ana's heart rose at the sight of her father on horseback, his royal robe streaming behind him, his face grim and determined. He angled his horse toward her and leaned over to one side, his gaze trained on her. Ana's eyes widened, instinctively knowing what he intended to do. She widened her stance and bent her knees slightly, her heart pounding as Father neared.

The ground trembled as he approached, and as he passed Ana, he leaned over and grabbed her, wrenching her from Maddoc's grip and using the momentum of his body and her push off the ground to flip her behind him on the horse. Ana tried to find something to cling to in order to maintain her balance, but she was facing the wrong direction and the copious layers of material on her dress were not suited to remain upright on a saddle.

A thunderous roar tore through the air, and Ana held onto her seat as her eyes met Maddoc's. She wanted to look away, to avoid being targeted with his fury, but she'd never been able to. Tearing his eyes away from her, he threw his whole body into fighting even more furiously against the king's guard, his sword moving at lightning speed as he dispatched of her father's most skilled men. As soon as he speared the last one, his bow was in his hands and an arrow was already flying toward her before he'd barely looked up.

Ana didn't have time to scream. The arrow zipped past her and she heard a grunt behind her, followed by a low gurgling groan. *No!*

~

Author Note

This story began as a silly question from my dad. Could I write a quick story inspired by a fairytale in a short time? The answer is a resounding NO! lol I tried, but this story was not quick, and it's not short, since it needed to span two books. It was also inspired by a folk tale (Robin Hood), not a fairytale, so basically, a fail all around, haha! That said, I really loved building this world and exploring the massive differences in personality and circumstances of Maddoc and Ana, and the power of status. The feel of this world is so different from Myth or Empire, and it was exciting figuring out how this disgraceful outlaw went about getting his princess.

I must say, I really missed writing in the male POV for this book :(Thankfully, the next book is more evenly balanced, and I know I'm going to have fun with Maddoc's rage and obsession lol

If I didn't have another series I need to get back to, I would have spent some time creating some of the "factual retellings" of Alpha and Omega stories Ana found in the library, complete with steamy diary entries and everything lol. But I don't have time. There are two other Omegas in this world, as mentioned, and one of them appears in the next book. So I might return to this world at a later time, and if I do, I'll make the retellings as an extra bonus for my Halos. Of course, you can read the full unabridged version of *The Lox Empire* in Crave To Conquer. :)

I hope you have enjoyed this book! If you know anyone else who would enjoy it, please recommend it to them. If you didn't enjoy it or felt that this couple wasn't for you, try my MYTH OF OMEGA series or my EMPIRE OF ANGELS series to see if one of those captures you. I also have a brand new series coming later this year, so hopefully, I can grab your interest in the future. Thanks so much for checking this one out, and please consider leaving a review wherever you bought the book, so other readers know what they're getting into if they decide to try it.

My reader's group Dark Halos is the best way to get news, bonuses, prizes, and also just to chat and drool over sexy bodies with me :p Some of the names in this book came from a call I put out for name suggestions in there so jump in and join us! :)

Acknowledgments

Randie: You are a beast! Thank you so much for all the hard work you put into this, your notes and comments are invaluable! If I get any block caps in the comments, I know I must be doing something right lol :) x

Margarita: What a random diversion this story was! Lol Thank you for being such a great sounding board and voice of unwavering support. You are amazing.

To my friends and family, you know the drill lol :) It will never change. Love you all immensely x

~ Zoey Ellis ~

About Zoey Ellis

Zoey Ellis writes dark, magical, fantasy romances about tortured, possessive, alpha anti-heroes and the sassy heroines who belong to them (even if they don't want to!). Filled with passionate, carnal steam, Zoey's stories feature couples that go through tough journeys and make mistakes but ultimately have to grow for each other to survive the dark worlds they inhabit.

Described as 'deliciously dark' and 'unputdownable', Zoey's thrilling, fantastical romances come complete with roller-coaster twists and turns, unique worlds, and happy endings.

Zoey is a Londoner, cat mama, and proud romance and epic fantasy addict. She loves jealous/possessive heroes, sexual tension that jumps off the page, and memorable, magical worlds. She reads most genres of romance and has a special love for the 'true mates' trope and dark angst.

Snoop around Zoey's online home for her favorite reads, release news, and bonus media about her fantasy worlds: www.zoeyellis.com

Made in the USA
Coppell, TX
04 December 2021

67159117R00111